ABOUT THE AUTHOR

Ada Cakalli is a British author.
In 2010 she graduated from Cardiff University with an
M.Sc. degree in structural engineering.
Ever since, she has been dividing her time between writing,
an early passion of hers, and working as an
engineer in London's corporate world.
She lives in Surrey with her husband and son.

ADA CAKALLI

HOMETOWN FENCES

A NOVEL

Published by
Elite Publishing Academy
www.elitepublishingacademy.co.uk

First Edition published 2020
© Ada Cakalli 2020

Printed and bound in Great Britain by
Elite Publishing Academy

A catalogue record for this book
is available from The British Library

ISBN 978-1912713-60-8

London, 21 December 2018 – Present Day

The night flight from London to Dubai was quiet. I could only remember around forty passengers boarding the large Airbus 380; an airplane that could easily accommodate seven times more people.

Soon after the airplane took off, most passengers wrapped themselves in blankets, and slowly, one after the other, subsided into long, undisturbed naps.

Looking at them like that, sleeping serenely above the skies, I felt as if I was looking at angels. Angels, with clipped wings, beneath dark blue blankets who were now taking a break from their everyday life in the skies.

I wanted to do the same, sleep innocently amongst them, but the thought of my recent trip to Great Falls Town wouldn't let me.

In a way, I was relieved that I had finally confronted some of the ghosts from my past, but the whole experience had left me feeling drained. So drained, that I could not sleep.

For years I had thought that my life was happening in my hometown, regardless of where I was living. My real life was happening there. What I was experiencing elsewhere was simply time passing. Things I saw and did in other places, people I met; none of these things mattered. My soul was trapped in the fences of that small town at the edge of the northern border of Vermont. A town, which most of the year was covered in thick layers of snow that preserved its secrets as well as they preserved its nature.

It was hard to let go of the fences, even as I grew older and stronger, even as I lived miles and miles away from home. They were always there, always on me.

Despite the heavy thoughts in my head about the events back home, I was still feeling happy to return to Dubai. Everything good that had ever happened to me was there. Everything that had made me want to be a better person, a person who saw light in the world. And if it hadn't been for that recent trip to Great Falls Town, I would have thought that my life was beginning to finally happen there. Now, I would need a good few months before I could feel sober again; sober from the pain and memories I had accumulated in the last few days.

I took a deep sigh, hoping to reduce the feeling of anxiety that had started to build up in my chest, and opened the window shade next to me.

I rested my head on a travel cushion that I had bought at London's Heathrow Airport and reassured myself that everything was going to be okay.

With all the angelic faces sleeping, the airplane felt very silent; almost like an empty hotel room. It wasn't just the people sleeping that made me think that; it was also the fact that the lights were off and the window shades had been closed, which made it difficult for me to see anything further than a seat away. To further add to that strange feeling of acuteness, the air hostesses had disappeared from sight.

I tried to focus my eyesight outside the window, in an effort to reduce the anxious butterflies now fluttering madly in my chest.

Squinting hard, I could see a faint light reflected from a distant star into the window. It was coming and going in short sequences, as if trying to deliver a

Morse coded message. God, I thought, if it wasn't for that enigmatic message coming from the universe, I would have thought that the plane was travelling through vacuum and someone twisted had placed angel like mannequins wrapped around blankets to keep me company.

But who knows, maybe I even liked it that way. The odd thing here was that deep down inside me, hidden under thin layers of everyday distractions, there still lied a faint urge to steal that feeling of vacuum; to live in it forever. I could then watch earth rotate slowly in the dark as I diminished in emptiness, undisturbed of the nonreturn point, where gravity gave way to the claws of universe.

Apart from the fragile, faint light buzzing with life, the sky looked otherwise dull. There were no other stars glittering brightly. Strangely though, it felt better that way, as the loneliness of the plane, wrapped up in darkness became far more striking.

Someone had told me once that God travelled with the light, and if you could not see light, you could not see him either. I was not sure I believed in God anymore, but I was certain there was something extraordinary in that ray of light. Could it be that someone had orchestrated that exclusive show, rehearsed for millions of years, just so that I could see it? And if so, was it because they wanted to tempt me to become an eternal spectator, like the dead looking angel faces in my cabin? Or was it because they wanted me to see that flickering light, which out of hundreds of airplane windows had chosen to enter into mine?

Before I could decide which way to answer my question, I felt a gentle tap on my shoulder.

'Miss Swift?

'Yes,' I said, trying to look calm after the sudden jump.

The air hostess in front of me had shiny white teeth, circled around a bright, red lipstick. Her smile was larger than her mouth, but she didn't mind it, she kept her mouth fully open. It was impossible to see her face in the dark, apart from the dinosaur smile which seemed to radiate through darkness.

'Miss Swift, I am so sorry to disturb you, but as you are one of our most valuable costumers, we would like to wish you Merry Christmas and offer you a gift on behalf of our crew.'

Her mouth opened up further and I could now see all her shiny teeth surrounded by a giant, red ring. She brought down carefully the seat tray and placed a plastic bowl in front of me.

'Some fresh figs in the bowl for you, with our compliments!'

I trembled and pushed the bowl back.

'Nooo. No figs, nooo.'

'Miss Swift, Miss Swift.' I heard the soft voice whispering from behind. I opened my eyes and before I could look up, she had brought her mouth close to my face.

'I am so sorry to disturb you Miss Swift; did I wake you up?' She said politely.

'Nooo, no problem, I wasn't sleeping.' I lied, and suddenly realized that a strange taste of figs was itching my throat. I couldn't remember the last time I had figs and frankly, I had almost forgotten how they tasted. However, the thought of them was horrific enough to make me vomit.

'I understand you may not wish to be disturbed at this time, but as you are one of our frequent flyers, and it is now Christmas season, we would like to thank you for flying with us. The cabin crew would like to offer free drinks and desserts for the rest of the flight. We do not have cake unfortunately; however, muffins and biscuits are available at the bar.'

I had noticed by then the red lipstick; however, the white teeth looked yellowish now and the smile was a quarter of the mouth. She did not look like a wicked clown anymore, but rather like a typical, middle aged woman with pale white skin, thin brown hair and comforting eyes.

'Oh, thank you very much. Sure, I will keep that in mind. I would rather have a blanket instead, if that is okay.' I said, smiling politely.

'Sure, Miss Swift, I will be right back. Enjoy the rest of the flight.' She whispered and moved off slowly.

'Thank you.' I said, with a light sigh.

I closed my eyes for a second to try and come to terms with what had happened. I was so relieved the dream air hostess had been replaced by a human. But I was also slightly upset with myself; I should have realized I had been dreaming. Her smile had been monstrous after all.

God, I felt so powerless over my dreams. They chose to distort reality the way they pleased. They flipped my mood the way they wanted, sometimes for the better, most times for the worst. I wished I could just get rid of them altogether.

Certain that I would not be able to go back to sleep, I thought that the best thing to do was review the presentation that I had received from the team in

Dubai the night before. In the morning, I would attend a meeting with the clients and I needed to be ready in case they fired any questions at me. We would present the progress of the "New Millennium" project and do a high-level risk assessment for all the activities planned for the New Year.

That was precisely what I was going to do, I thought. I had three more hours to go. I would not look at the angelic mannequins around me and I would most definitely not glance at any air hostesses passing by. It wouldn't be that hard, I was sure.

I would keep the window open and hope for more light to come through as the minutes went by.

The day ahead was going to be brilliant, I told myself, still feeling anxious inside.

Slightly unconvinced, I repeated in my head the same thing again, this time with my eyes closed, but the anxious butterflies had no intention of leaving my chest.

I opened my eyes, and before I could glance again at the ray of light outside the window, I felt the taste of figs still itching my throat.

About one year ago, London, 12 December 2017

I always wondered why companies chose to buy the exact same set of pencils for their employees. Every time they chose the ones with black and yellow stripes, every single time. It baffled me, to say the least.

If you placed those pencils in a row, they would all look the same, like faceless little soldiers. If you swapped the second pencil with the fifth, I could bet a fiver that no one would tell the difference. You could color the stripes, scratch down your name, eat the rubber, damage the metallic cover at the bottom, tippex white lines around the circumference; use the sharpener in some of them; they would still look the same. And if you used the sharpener to the extent that you did not need a pencil any more, the row of rigid pencils would rigorously remain constant.

I knew this to be true as I had tested it. At the beginning of the year I would place eight pencils in a row at the side of my desk. As time passed, people would come by and borrow a pencil. Some of them would return it back, some would forget and some would return new pencils. The row looked exactly the same though, black and yellow stripes at the side of my desk.

A day earlier, before leaving work, I had placed them in a straight row at the edge of my desk, disciplined line of soldiers as they were, always watching my back. The janitor had moved them in the evening, so now, they were scattered around my table, like heroes in a lost battlefield.

'Good morning, Sharron.' My boss yelled, lifting his right hand in the air while walking past me, as if trying to show me something in the distance. 'Meeting at ten today...Please, send out an invite.'

'Yes, of course. What meeting, sorry?' I said, as I tried to put my soldiers back in line.

'The interview for the "New Millennium" project manager position! I thought I mentioned it yesterday. Oh well, maybe I didn't. Anyways, please prepare the files by nine thirty as I need to review them and please turn on the heating in the room, it gets quite chilly in there.'

'Yes, of course Reza, I will send the invitation now.' I said confidently, fully aware that he had not mentioned anything about an interview the day before.

I printed out the CV of the candidate and a list of standard questions for myself.

My line manager, Reza Farkhai liked to invite engineers to attend job interviews. He said it helped build up confidence and improve leadership skills. Normally, I would sit at the table alongside him and other managers and would write down the candidate's answers to the questions. I was also entitled to ask a list of standard questions, which Reza had pre-approved. That gave me particular joy, as I felt I was not a mere typing machine. After the meeting, Reza would sit down with me and score the answers. At sixty-three, he did not recall most of the conversations we had during such meetings, hence he needed an assistant to write them down. The scoring process was straightforward. I summarized each answer and after a short discussion with him, we agreed on a final score.

Despite his turbulent memory, Reza seemed to enjoy the interviews and talked a lot about the industry, finance, and even politics with the candidates. This he could do only when other managers were not present in the room and felt relaxed enough to have an informal chat with them. I had a feeling that those particular interviews felt like a journey to his youth and home country; a world that did not exist outside the room. The nostalgia of his childhood, years back, in the pre-revolutionary Iran seemed to almost define the flow of the conversations. At this age, it became more pronounced, as if the memories tried to take over his present life.

I had come to know Reza quite late in his career. Thirty years ago, he had been the shining star of the geotechnical department. Now with age, a kidney operation and the department shrinking to four people, he had lost interest in work.

At 10 a.m. sharp, HR manager Catherine Baker entered the room followed by the new candidate. Catherine had a Barbie type beauty, long, blonde hair and a tall, skinny figure, which gave her a lot of confidence when talking to people. The truth is, I had not met anyone that did not feel intimidated by her looks at the beginning of an interview.

She introduced us to the candidate with the usual giggling and excessive politeness that followed each time she opened her mouth, as her floor slamming heels finally decided to take a rest.

'Good morning, Reza. This is Liam Monroe. Reza is the structures geotechnical manager and Sharron Swift is a civil engineer working with him on the "New Millennium" project. Aaron Sealy and Simon Howell, the line managers of the project will join us on the phone from Dubai.'

We shook hands and sat down. As we were waiting for the team in Dubai to dial in, I began to think I had never met someone with that surname.

Like most people, I had a fascination with Marilyn Monroe, not just with her looks, but her story too. Liam Monroe was a disappointment in that respect; he bore no physical resemblance with Marilyn. That is not to say he was unattractive though. He was rather handsome, and from what I could see, he did not acknowledge that, which was something I appreciated in people, as they were the ones who truly understood the difference between a blessing and an asset.

Apart from his appealing face, there was nothing else special about him, at least physically. And, like with most candidates, I had not bothered to read his CV. There was no point after all, they all exaggerated about their experience and lied about their skills.

'Mr. Monroe, you understand this interview is for a very important role in the organization, as we are trying to consolidate our presence in the Middle East. As a construction project manager in the "New Millennium" project, you could oversee up to forty employees and six subcontractors. We are planning to conduct a second round of interviews before Christmas with a selected number of applicants.' Reza explained without much enthusiasm.

'Yes, I am aware of that.' Liam Monroe said, turning his head towards me, as I started to type on the laptop.

I used to feel very uncomfortable when people saw me writing down their answers, but I had got over it with time, so I did not mind any preconceptions.

Catherine began to explain more about the role, the hours of work and expat package. To my surprise, Liam Monroe remained completely switched on during their conversation. He made some good points and asked her a couple of questions. Catherine was

12

left slightly irritated by his sharpness and cut him off after a few questions.

As the interview progressed, I started to notice his hands. Liam Monroe had beautiful, long fingers that tingled lightly when rested on the desk.

I also noticed that he knew his stuff but lacked eloquence. That, in my view, was not a bad thing. I personally liked his lack of articulation; most managers spoke like solicitors during interviews.

Despite my sense of curiosity towards him, primarily aimed at his wittiness, Liam did not show any signs of reciprocation. He paid little attention to me. Probably he had realized I was too unimportant to have a say in the decision-making process. Or maybe my typing simply distracted him. He only looked at Reza, who seemed to enjoy their conversation, which most certainly was due to Liam Monroe's unwieldy nature, but also due to his sharp and brief answers.

Half an hour through the interview, Reza began to look at my paper, a signal that my turn to ask a question had come.

'Any questions from you, Sharron?' He asked with a tired voice, as if telling me to keep it short.

'Hmm, yes, of course. So, what is your aspiration in life?' I said and grabbed the black and yellow striped pencil from inside my notebook.

'My aspiration, hmm, is to live, I suppose a… a purposeful life. I would like to be able to change my life for the better; not just my life but the lives of others around me, I suppose. I want to be able to make a difference, that sort of thing.' He said thoughtfully, surprised and rather disappointed he had not come up with a more articulated answer.

I nodded and put my head down. A firm knot spread viciously on my throat and blocked the airway, until I felt I could breathe no more.

Why were people so obsessed with making a difference, I thought? What if you weren't able to make a difference or didn't want to? What if you were a black and yellow striped pencil with nothing to stand out from the crowd? What was wrong with that? What was wrong with having no aspirations?

I rushed to give away a smile but due to anxiety it turned out like an odd sneer, further boosting the awkwardness in the room. At that point, Reza's swift intuition intervened to save the day.

'All right, ladies and gentlemen. I think we do not need to ask further questions for now. We should call it a day. Let's have some coffee. The kitchen is just around the corner. Shall we, Liam?'

'Yes, thank you.' Liam Monroe said, relieved from the trap question I had set up for him.

I didn't move from my seat. I had a sip of water when everyone had left and then pretended to close out paperwork on the laptop. When I felt better, I sneaked quietly out of the room. As I was about to sit down at my desk, Reza came out of the kitchen and asked me to join them.

A few minutes later, I walked in the kitchen to see Liam Monroe trying to figure out how to turn on the espresso machine. As I got nearer, I noticed he was a bit chubbier than I had thought originally.

The light blue eyes and soft white face radiated clarity and honesty. Around thirty-five, he looked older due to his posture and clumsiness. I thought he was most likely a kind person and that his answer had in fact been a generic statement about life, not a personal attack.

'Do you need milk? This espresso is too heavy... I always have mine with milk.' I said, as I turned on the espresso machine.

'Thanks for that. I haven't really used an espresso machine before.' He said apologetically, looking at the well-hidden espresso machine button I had just pressed. 'I'll try it with some milk, thank you.'

'Okay, no problem... You know, you have an odd surname. I suppose you are not related to Marilyn Monroe?' I joked, in a forced attempt to sound friendlier.

'Oh no, I am not that fortunate, not as fortunate as her, that is.' He smiled and took a step closer to me.

'You think she was fortunate?' I asked, my chest now fluttering. 'Do you know how she died?'

'She killed herself, right?' He said bluntly, like a happy child does when knowing the answer to a simple history question.

'Yes, you are right, she did eventually.' I said, smiling with disappointment.

I turned my back to him and walked towards the fridge. As I turned around, I realized that he let out a light sigh. I smiled again, this time politely, handed him the milk and walked away in silence, leaving him looking awkwardly guilty from yet another trap question.

That afternoon, I heard from Reza that Liam Monroe would be offered the job.

London, Friday, 20 December 2017 - Evening

I left work early as I knew it was about to happen soon. It was the last weekend before Christmas, so I did not have much time.

At work, I cleaned up my desk and tidied up the project folders for Reza to read through in the morning. I responded to all outstanding emails and filed all of them in the public folders for Reza to be able to find them.

I then collected the office shoes from under the desk and put them cautiously in the clothes recycling bin. I emptied the drawers and threw all the sweets, toiletries and personal files that were there to the office bin.

Before leaving, I glued the pencils, all eight of them, set in a straight row, at the side of the desk. I carved a letter on each of their skins; a way of christening them with an identity. The cleaning lady would clean off the glue in the evening and probably bin them too.

In the best case, they would remain glued on the desk for a week or so and eventually disappear in different parts of the building, scattered around people's desks and drawers. No one would ever realize what the tattooed letters on their skin had meant or that they had been someone's comrade, their only friend. Poor, brothers in arms, I thought. Simply because they were born with the exact same face as million others, no one bothered to spot their individuality, their unique ability to craft letters and numbers. No one would ever miss those pencils because they were not made to look great, but rather be great.

By the time I arrived home, it was dark outside. I felt a great relief I was inside my own, little castle. I turned on the water heater, quickly removed the coat and headed to the fridge. The champagne bottle was waiting for me, pink and fruity, ready to celebrate. I opened it carefully and poured some in a champagne glass, then walked to the living room and sat lazily on the couch. It was very comforting to be on my own after a long day at work.

The couch was positioned in front of the balcony, from where I could see a busy street flourishing with shops and restaurants. Mothers, holding their children by the hand, walked hastily out of glittery shops, carrying large Christmas presents.

Young couples enjoyed slow strolls, unperturbed by the December cold. An old man, with moldy, black clothes and a white, long beard that resembled Santa's, stood behind a grey, 19th century statue and sang a mysterious song. I guessed for a moment and picked a song. There it was: 'Last Christmas'. It fit him perfectly.

Gazing at the view for a good half hour from my living room couch, I realized that I would miss that happy, suburban, South West London neighborhood. It was always full of happy strangers going somewhere, actors in a film with no end or beginning, thrown in a set with the sole purpose of keeping me company.

I took a sip of champagne. It was cold and refreshing and gave me the chills. As I continued to drink, I noticed that little ice was left on both sides of the street, a reminder that Christmas was best celebrated with snow. Flashbacks of memories passed through my eyes every time I saw patches of snow in

London. It brought back angels and demons from the past, fighting in turn to dominate the present.

The lights from the shops that penetrated through the balcony glass door, left red and green shadows dancing on the grey carpet floor. In my mind, there was no doubt that Christmas was the best time of the year, a time when people got together and prepared rich meals, made with love. It was truly about love and sharing with one another. It was humanity's best expression of its legacy in the world; the legacy of kindness and uncompromised love. Many years ago, I had believed in that legacy. Christie and I would hand out cookies cut in the shapes of snowmen, Santa Claus and stars to bypassers, outside her father's restaurant. We would volunteer to shovel the snow from the house driveways of the elderly. Together with Father George, we would distribute soup to the homeless at St. Thomas church and do a lot more. But then things changed. The world got mad and the demons defeated the angels.

I rubbed my hands against my eyes to clean up the tears and sipped a little more champagne. It tasted like heaven. Luckily, the room was clean and tidy, just as I had left it in the morning. No dishes to clean, no clothes to iron. It was as if the apartment had planned it all before me.

I took the phone out of the bag and began to scroll through messages. Firstly, I read the daily texts from my little brother Bob, asking about my health and if work was going well. Then I continued on to mother's texts. She asked all sorts of things like: Was I taking my medication? Had I met anyone interesting? Did I go to the gym? I read some fifteen texts and put the phone down. The more I read, the worse it got. I sipped more champagne and turned my head towards the balcony door. The view from the street did nothing to entertain me.

I realized the bathtub would be filled with water by then, so I returned to the bathroom and turned the tap off. I then walked to the room, put some music on the radio and removed all of my clothes. I folded them neatly and hid them under clean laundry in the wardrobe. The bathroom was filled with hot steam when I returned, so I lied down slowly in the bathtub, silently humming the lyrics from the song "Losing my religion" that was being played on the radio. There, under water, my head throbbed with self-doubt. What if I failed again? What if it all went terribly wrong? No, I would not fail myself again. Not this time, for sure not this time, I told myself.

I stayed like that for an hour, my face under the water, my mind playing different ending scenarios. At some point, I realized the bath was taking too long. Scared of my numbness, I decided to act. I knew the longer I thought about it, the more complex the process would be, so I got up, covered myself in a towel and walked quickly back to the living room. Playing hide and seek with my fears for all my adult life had weakened me to the point I had given up. I could not fight any more. I needed to let go. It was my only chance for peace, the only chance to escape the permanent stagnation.

The adrenaline picked up as I approached the cupboard. My heartbeat accelerated in protest, leaving my hands trembling with fear. I opened the drawer and took out the box. Then I sat down on the floor, numb, not able to move. I tried to convince myself that it had to be done quickly, as it was the only way out, the only route to escape. I did not have any doubts, no, yet I was scared, like never before.

My fingers searched attentively through the box until they reached the pills. Tears rushed through my eyes, onto my cheeks and mouth.

Sitting there in the dark, I wept in silence, squeezing the pills on my palms, on a last, hopeless call for regret. I then counted them; the correct number I needed to take, forty.

As I stood up, I noticed the lights from the street had become more vivid so I walked to the glass door and opened it slightly for fresh air. The street was full of life, yet it felt remotely distant. I loved that street; I wished I could be like anyone out there. But I wasn't. I did not have the option to get a train to the future like they did. Maybe I had that option once, but had somehow lost the ticket. I was only left with a ticket to the past.

And that train never missed its destination; it always travelled back to the same old place, to the same old smell. I knew, I could not stop it; but I could jump from it.

That was precisely what I was going to do. I put on my clean pajamas, turned the phone off, gripped the champagne glass and moved back to the bedroom. I lied down in bed, silently breathing in fresh air and forcing it out.

I took the pills slowly, but steadily, sipping champagne to sweeten the taste. There, in my bed, hidden under the quilt, I did not feel sadness or terror, but rather wonder. What would happen next? Where would I go, what would I do? Heaven surely did not smell of figs, I thought, as the lights from the street began to vanish.

About ten years ago, Great Falls Town, 02 December 2007

Winter came slowly but firmly to Great Falls Town. It covered the valleys and mountains, the forests and houses with its white mantel, as if to prove it had full control over the town's life.

Most of my friends did not like winter. It made them feel sad because in that small town of ours, right in the northern borders of Vermont, there was nowhere to go, nothing to do. They preferred summer, when the town got a lot more vibrant, due to the many tourists that flocked in from all around the country to swim in the lake. I, on the contrary, loved winter and everything that came with it; the serenity of the mountains, wrapped in whiteness, the loneliness of the frozen lake and the hubbub of the little town center, which was the only, warm bubble of life in that huge desert of ice.

I loved winter partly because I could spend more time with myself, dreaming about things I would do when I grew up but primarily because I could hang out with Christie, my best friend in the whole world. During winter, she had more time to spend with me after school, as there was less to do at her father's restaurant.

Christie Jones and I first met at pre-school, when we were both four. Christie was the tall, strong girl everyone was afraid of, and I was the short, weak girl everyone bullied. We bonded as kids when she once beat a boy that teased me for being too skinny.

Through elementary school, Christie took me under her wing, as I was constantly bullied for being small and weak. At fourteen, I started to grow taller and stronger, but never managed to catch up with her. Now, at sixteen, she was still the pretty, tall, blonde girl and I was still everything she wasn't.

'Good morning, Mr. Jones', I said, rubbing my hands to keep warm as I walked into the restaurant that felt like my second home.

'Good Morning, my dear. How are you today? Come quickly to the fire. Did you mother drop you?'

'No, I took the bicycle. It is freezing out there; I almost slid a couple of times. The road is packed in snow. The police patrol mentioned the road to Oakwood Hills is blocked; do you still think you'll be able to get the trees tonight?'

'Don't worry, I will get them tonight, the best spruces in town, you'll see. Now, sit down, put those frostbitten fingers near the fire. I will make you a toast. Christie is upstairs; she is helping in the kitchen.' He said and walked slowly towards the kitchen door.

Paradise Restaurant was a small, cozy restaurant situated in the heart of Great Falls Town, next to the Iowa lake. It was a favorite, due to its location and good service. The Jones family had run the business for three generations and had successfully managed to maintain a good name throughout the years. Three people worked full time in the restaurant, Mrs. Elliott - the cook, and two waiters - twin brothers Tom and Nick - who seemed to also be doing everything else. There were always people in the restaurant and I was familiar with most of them.

At this time of year, people would go out to the town center, do their Christmas shopping and stop by the restaurant for a warm soup or chocolate cake.

Like most people in town, I loved the place, the mixture of aromas, the view of the lake, the humming of people and the warmth of the fireplace. Above all, I loved Christie, my sister, my best friend in the entire world.

'You nutter, did you ride in the snow?' Christie yelled as she walked hastily down the stairs. I nodded and gave her a long, excited smile. I hadn't seen her for three days, as school had been closed due to heavy snow, and my mother had refused to drive to the town center.

Christmas time was always busy at our house. My mother would cook for days, different recipes of cakes and tarts. She would wash the curtains, the blankets, the bed sheets and everything else that could hold germs.

Since my parents' divorce six years ago, grandmother would come over to Great Falls Town to spend Christmas with us. That meant the house had to go through a hysterical cleaning expedition.

During the fierce cleaning days, I would normally look after my young brother Bob and occasionally help mother in the kitchen. That's what I had been doing for the past three days and I had become extremely bored. Trapped in the house, as the snow continued to fall, I had missed my time with Christie. I had imagined how exciting Paradise Restaurant would have been; Mr. Jones decorating the front windows with shimmering lights, Mrs. Elliott baking heart melting cookies full of chocolate and white sugar and Christie talking to customers, dressed in her glittering Christmas jumper. Now that I was there, it felt even better, like a dream come true. I could smell the buttery flavors coming from the kitchen as I sat near the fireplace, craving in silence for a creamy cake.

I had secretly prayed for Christie to bring some of the freshly baked Vanilla cakes when Mr. Jones had gone in the kitchen to call her, but she hadn't. She had just rushed out in a hurry. At least she was wearing her Christmas jumper, just like I had thought she would.

Christie sat next to me and gave me a long, warm hug. 'Thank God you made it safely. You should not be riding in the snow, you crazy girl. Did you get sick and tired of nannying Bobby?'

'Yes, I did. I have been watching Disney movies for three long days.' I said, annoyed, and smacked my lips to reinforce that.

'Oh, that is perfect; I wish I could do the same. I have been working full time. Dad asked me to help Father George set up a buffet in the church for St. Patrick's orphanage and then, the work over here has been insane. I don't know where to begin. I've got loads to tell you… First things first, do you want some hot chocolate? You must be freezing.'

I nodded shyly as Christie made a theatrical sign to Tom to bring the usual drinks.

'I have got some good news for you.' She continued, whispering the words secretively into my ear.

'What news, what's happened in three days?' I said, surprised of what I had just heard.

'It has been going on for a while now, but I wanted to find the right time to tell you. I have met someone.'

'What? Who? Someone from school?' I asked, raising my voice unconsciously.

'Hush, no, not from school. Someone older.' She said and smiled, her cheeks popping up with amusement.

'Who is that?' I persisted, puzzled and intrigued at the same time.

'I won't tell you yet, give me some time. But I can tell you *this*, he is very interesting, unlike the boys at school. He is different, he is truly genuine.'

'What are you talking about? What does the word "genuine" mean, anyways? Did you hear that word from one of your customers here? I don't think you can use that word to describe people, silly. Anyways, tell me, how did you meet him?' I asked briskly, my heart pounding fast.

'Let's sit down by the window', she said, pointing at the far end of the restaurant, pretending to not have heard my derogatory comment about the word "genuine".

I nodded with discontent, coughing nervously as we walked through the restaurant. Christie sat down on the chair facing the main hall, her eyes vividly scanning the space around us for intruders.

'Tell me now - where did you meet him? You have a crush on him, right?' I asked, irritated by the whole mystery thing. I had felt left out of her new secret, a serious new secret.

'I think I like him, but I am not sure how much, at this point. Anyways, what did my grandma always say? 'Only love keeps the world going.'

'Oh right, since when did you become a love expert? Tell me, how much older is he? He is not creepy old, is he?'

'No Sharrie, he is not creepy old. For God's sake, give me some time. Don't be so pushy. I'll tell you in a week or so. Let's see how things turn out.'

She looked away and started to flicker her fingers on the table. She did that when she was nervous, it was her impatience release valve. But this time she looked oddly muted. I had never seen her like that. Something had happened to her, something strange. She had become nervous, secretive. It seemed as if we had not seen each other for many years and had all of a sudden arranged a meeting to discuss in a formal, business-like way our present lives. We were having the sort of conversations grownups had. The sort where you don't tell too much, and the stuff you tell is always brushed with polite fakeness.

I knew Christie was a good observer; the work at the restaurant had helped her pick up mannerisms, patterns in people's behavior and adopt them as her own. She now looked like a sophisticated lady sitting in front of a child, trying to engage in a comprehensive conversation about life. Unfortunately, I was the child in that conversation.

'Please, just tell me where you met him and how long you have been seeing him.' I begged, as a child would. 'I promise I will never ask anything about him again, if you tell me.'

'Ok, fine. I met him around here. I have been seeing him for hmm, four weeks now.' She said hesitantly and crossed her arms over her chest. Tom had just emerged, carrying the hot chocolates, a large toast for me and two plates of Vanilla cake. I remained silent until he left.

My appetite for the buttery cake had evaporated by then. 'Oh god, four weeks? And you said nothing all this time? I thought we did not have secrets. Do I know him? At least tell me that.'

She shook her head while biting her lower lip. She then put the hands back on the table and continued in her role of a sophisticated lady.

'He is just a friend, Sharron, don't make it sound like a big deal. He is not a pervert or anything like that, trust me.' She said and sipped the hot chocolate. 'Now, have some cake. When is Grandma coming over?'

I grimaced. She was still treating me like a child.

'She will be here next week, so everything has to be perfect by then. I wish I was nine, like Bob, and did not have to worry about her visit. She will take my room, you see, so I have scrubbed and polished every single item in there. I have removed all Akon posters.'

Christie burst into loud laughs. She then changed her voice in a strenuous effort to mock my grandma's. 'Christie, dear, have you done your homework? Sharron needs to study more; her chemistry grades are low.'

I couldn't help but join her laugh. Christie was back to her true self, the charming, happy and loving girl she had always been. My bestie, my sister. If only we could stay in that moment forever.

Christie was not really made for books. That was the reason grandma was always worried about her influence over me. She didn't exactly hate school; she just found it boring. Mr. Jones had never shown interest to know her grades or scolded her when she didn't do well in an exam. He knew that school was not one of her fortes, as Christie often said. That was the reason why he never came to any of the parent-teacher meetings either. For a small town like ours, that was not unusual; Mr. Jones knew all of our teachers and met them regularly at the restaurant. My mother always said he avoided such meetings as he didn't want to feel let down by Christie's grades, but I knew the truth. He didn't want to upset her by being there. The thing was, Mr. Jones never really saw Christie going to college. Even when my mother had once suggested we, girls could move together to the same college after high school, he had nodded lethargically, mumbling that Christie was free to study anything and anywhere she wanted. In all cases, he would pay her fees. I didn't know if he was being honest or not, as they were both ambiguous whenever the topic of education was brought up. It was as if they had a silent pact; she could do anything she wanted when she grew up, as long as she continued to look after the restaurant.

That didn't seem to bother Christie though. After three generations in the restaurant business, she had made up her mind to follow in the steps of the family and seemed to have no regrets about that. She knew that she would also have to look after Mr. Jones eventually, as she was his only child. That had made the decision even easier for her, or at least, that is what she had told me once.

Mr. Jones had heard the occasional bursts of laughter and was now approaching the table shyly. His long, slim figure, was more pronounced when he walked.

Vince Jones was a good man, generous and kind. In fact, more generous than most people I had met in my life.

He would invite anyone for a soup or drink at his restaurant, be it a homeless man sitting on a bench across the street, a lost tourist, or an old couple visiting the lake; they were all welcome at his restaurant. And they were all treated like good, old friends. I looked up to him for that.

The only thing I did not quite like about Mr. Jones was his once in a while, authoritative behavior. But that again was understandable, considering the fact that he was a single parent. Mrs. Jones had passed away when Christie was two and he had raised his daughter on his own. He had to be the strict and the tolerant parent at the same time, the good and the bad cop as they say. Deep inside though, the dreadful loss of his better half had not turned him into a bitter man; on the contrary, he had become more loving and caring of Christie and her friends. He would spoil her with whatever she asked for, from the latest smartphones to branded clothes none of her friends had. Each week she would get more pocket money than I would for the entire month.

Despite having a lot of material stuff, Christie was not a spoiled teenager. She had spent her entire childhood in the restaurant, helping her father run the place. Throughout the years, during good and bad times, she had been his rock. Now at sixteen, Christie was in charge of the finances and supply orders. She was practically in charge of the business. And of course, she was doing a bit of everything else too.

She cleaned up the floors and windows, watered the plants, moved tables and chairs around and assisted customers. Work gave her joy, a lot more joy than hanging out with friends or being at school would.

And she never complained about having to wake up daily at 5:30 a.m. to receive the supply orders, or staying up late when the restaurant was busy. Maybe that small restaurant, at the lips of Great Falls Town's lake was a little more than her father's business; it was also her home.

I usually felt that the days at the restaurant were long but happy for Christie; however, there were times when a dense cloud of melancholy covered her face. You could tell by the frowned eyebrows, the silence, the turbulent look, as if looking but not seeing.

It was tiredness, I had thought initially, but with time I realized that it was something more; it was nostalgia for an unlived childhood, a warm motherly hug. I wondered many times if Mr. Jones had ever noticed her cloudy days, when he stood by his chosen table, right next to the great fireplace, overlooking the peaceful lake waves pound on the rocky shore. Now, when Christie was almost sixteen, I was sure he had not.

'Are you girls enjoying the drinks? I will take the van to McAlester's shop shortly, to get the spruce.' He said, glancing at his watch, as if to confirm the time.

'Can we join you?' Christie asked. 'I would like to choose it myself.'

'Yes, can we join you, please?' I added, as excited as Christie.

Mr. Jones gave me an apologetic smile. 'I am sorry, girls; I think I should go on my own. The road is full of ice, it is best you stay here.'

'Dad, please.' Christie insisted. 'I have been working all day. I need some fresh air.'

'Please let us come with you; it's only a ten-minute drive away. We would really like to help you choose the right Christmas tree. I rode all this way for that.' I added, always eager to support Christie.

Mr. Jones sighed. 'All right, come on then. But you will help me carry it to the van.'

'Sure, we will. Give me a second.' Christie said and ran furiously up to the kitchen. A minute later, she was back carrying a large box of sweets, wrapped delicately in a blue, decorative foil. 'Let's go Sharrie, hurry up." She yelled at me across the room, as she stood right next to the exit door.

'Coming, coming.' I yelled back, trying to remember where I had left my coat and gloves.

A few seconds later, I was fired up and ready to go. 'Hmm, I can smell almond biscuits,' I said, as I got closer to Christie. 'Who's the gift box for?'

'For Mr. McAlester. Father George told me he is better now; he's returned to the shop.' She said and gave me a reassuring smile.

'That's good. Poor, old man. It's cancer, right?'

'Thyroid tumor.' She said, pouting her lips with sadness.

By working at the restaurant, Christie had learnt that a warm biscuit, served alongside the morning tea, would bring smiles to people's faces. She knew that a small gift could pull people's hearts together, and now was doing just that.

I kept the door open to let Christie walk out and as I prepared to take a step forward, I caught a glimpse of Mrs. Elliott, walking down the kitchen stairs, with a freshly baked Christmas cake on her hands. She gave me a big, cheerful smile, her white, big teeth shining like giant pearls, the red lipstick radiating like fire across the room. I closed the door behind me, waving at her, and walked to the van in high spirits.

Mr. Jones turned the radio on, as I squeezed myself to sit beside Christie, on the front seat.

We drove slowly on the winding road, carefully avoiding patches of packed snow. Christie kept the biscuits box steady on her leap, as she played with radio channels. I had my eyes locked on the window, gazing in admiration at the valley below our feet.

As the car lurched up the hill, tiny Christmas lights from the houses deep down the valley, twinkled in the distance, shyly piercing the ghostly whiteness of snow. A Christmassy song started to play on the radio and Christie's croaky voice almost completely overran the singer.

My eyes were still cast on the window, watching the tall trees around us sleep peacefully under snow petals, like sleeping beauties waiting to be woken up by love.

We never made it to Mr. McAlester's shop. The car slipped on the last turn of the hill, sliding across the road safety barrier, onto the steep slope of the valley. It bounced and rolled until it finally crashed into a tall spruce, like a mad prince, brutally shaking his sleeping beauty.

The music on the radio never stopped. It kept playing, even when we banged fiercely into the tree, even when I lost consciousness. It was there, an echoing Christmassy sound in my ears, an anchor to the living world.

That day changed our lives forever. It was an ill omen of what was about to follow.

London, 21 December 2017

I had lost consciousness. I could not recall what had happened. I was not a ghost yet, no, I couldn't be. That didn't seem right, I was in pain. Ghosts didn't feel pain, did they? It felt like humanly pain, pain of the flesh.

The surrounding felt familiar too. I was in my bed, buried under the quilt, my hands on my stomach. Ah yes, the stomach. It was coming from there. The pain, my god, the pain, a million grenades exploding loudly in my stomach.

The noise from the top floor was getting louder. Some kind of music was playing in the background; it hit through my head like a knife-edged hammer, slicing the forehead into tiny pieces. I opened my eyes and realized it was still dark in the room, the curtains half open, the red and green lights from the street protruding the blackness with innocence. I wasn't gone yet. Music had saved me. For the second time. My anchor to the living world, I thought, as I closed my eyes.

The pain was unbearable. I wanted to vomit, to clutch my stomach. I couldn't though, as the spasms became more debilitating, each time I moved a muscle. I could feel the weight of the quilt over my belly; it was heavy and hot. My body was burning up like a piece of wood tossed in a hell furnace. I needed fresh air. I had to move that bloody quilt off me. I opened my mouth and took a shallow breath, just enough to buy some time.

It streamed through my neck, all the way to the stomach. Another spasm hit me then, bursting inside my tummy like bonfire. I could feel the stink of vomit from the stomach, yet I couldn't throw up. It was stuck inside my abdomen like hot lava eating up the crust of a volcano. I realized instinctively that I needed to act fast if I were to have a slim chance to escape the suffering. I flinched. The quilt came off my shoulders. The cold December air rushed through my body and it somehow stimulated my senses. The music felt louder this time. It was there, in the room; I just needed to follow it.

I pulled the quilt with my fingers down to my belly, blinking laboriously. I stretched my right leg out of the bed and forced my body to turn. I then bent over the edge of the bed and pushed myself down. I plunged into the ground like a dying whale, my stomach bursting like an erupting volcano, my face mashed on the floor. The ceramic tiles felt frosty on my cheeks. I gave myself a minute or so to pull myself together. The cold tiles, somehow, lightened the nausea and enhanced my senses. I crawled and slithered desperately, until I reached the apartment front door.

There were voices coming from the corridor, I could hear them. They seemed real. They had to be real. My nails scratched and scored the door paint, in a hopeless bid for hope.

I tried and tried, until I could not see any more, until my fingers became numb. The vigor of human flesh could not keep up with the stamina of the soul. It was over. My hands had given up. I rested my face on the floor, powerless, defeated. I contemplated death like never before. I murmured the word, for the very first time. Someone had played a last, crooked joke on me, to torment my body, to undignify my only act of heroism in life. I could end it there. I could let go. But then, I thought, it would be really pathetic to be found like that in the morning. Stinking of vomit, lying on the corridor floor, not even on my bed? I could imagine the horror on that person's face, as they tried to open the door, my body blocking the way like a bin bag.

Who knew death would turn out to be so vulgar? There was no pride in what I had done, no heroism. It was painful, foolish and embarrassing. My god, it was such a disappointment. It was as if the screenwriter had twisted the plot of a film to have a stupid, ordinary finale, so dull and dumb, I could laugh at it. It was total crap, too humiliating to even put it into words.

It couldn't be me; it couldn't be my life wasted like that. I closed my eyes and torturously whispered a weak 'Help'. Then I stopped, breathed in some air and whispered again. Then again and again. Until I stopped. Until it was over.

London, 22 December 2017

Bob was sitting on a chair by the window, flipping through a brochure or magazine, seemingly distracted. His dark brown eyes were moving slowly through the colorful pages. He wasn't reading, I could tell, he was merely looking at the pictures.

I noticed he was wearing the red T-shirt I had bought for him last summer, which was a bit small in size. I could never get his size right. He was growing up so fast, I thought.

Bob had most probably been waiting in the room for a few hours, as the plastic cup of coffee on the table next to him was empty. Since when did he drink coffee, anyways? Every time we went out, he would order orange juice or some energy drink. He would never drink coffee or tea. Surely, he had felt an urge for caffeine, considering the many hours he had been sitting in the room, or maybe he just wanted to feel a bit older, to feel a bit like me. That is what young siblings always do.

I was really glad he was there. I could see his thin arms leaning forward as he was reading, the short, black hair cuddling his forehead. We had the same black hair, soft and fine, like cat hair. When we were young, we would never use a comb. We didn't need it. Our hair was never tangled. We would go swimming in the pool and after a few hours of rest in the sun, our hair would become straight and shiny, like salon hair. It was funny I could remember such a blissful detail from our childhood, a few hours after I had attempted to wipe out all memories of him. But then, that was just human nature, I thought. We were genetically modeled to erase pain from our minds. Like antibodies suffocate a disease, the brain suffocates pain. We would otherwise not be able to carry on living.

Bob and I understood each other very well, better than we ever understood our parents, or they understood us. We were very close, perhaps because I was a lot older, and he tried to mimic me in everything.

He would listen to the same music, eat the same food, even like or dislike the same people in town as I did. I had shaped his character, I liked to think; like a sculptor does with a block of granite.

Sitting in the corner of the hospital room, Bob seemed awfully tired. His eyes were sagging down with despair, almost begging for sleep. Surprisingly, he did not seem panicked or sad. I could tell by the way he was flipping the pages; slowly, almost delicately. If my condition were unstable, he would be flipping the pages hastily, his eyebrows would be frowned. If I were too unwell, he would not be reading at all. Most likely, he would be sitting next to my bed, crying his eyes out. Watching him like that, calm and tired, gave me some reassurance that I was out of serious danger. But I didn't want to talk to him just yet. I preferred to go back to sleep. I needed to feel stronger, before I could face him. Not that he would buy any of my stories. But then, that was not my problem. It was my life at the end of the day. I chose how to live it and how to leave it.

Oh God, I did not mean that, did I? No, no, I didn't, I was just being an arrogant twat. My poor, baby brother. What had I done to him? I had ruined his life. For years and years, I had dragged him into my endless wars with the past. And he stood quiet by my side; never giving up on me, never questioning why it was cruel to mass produce black and yellow striped pencils. Or why it was bad to be very ambitious in life... What a tragedy for an eighteen-year-old to have to spend his life gripping his old sister, each time she decided to give up on herself.

As I closed my eyes, I got a rapid glimpse from Bob, striking through my eyelids like lightning.

'Sharrie, you awake?' He muttered, as he stood up from the chair. 'Sharron, hey, how are you feeling?' He continued, this time holding my hand. 'I'll call the doctor.' He said with a trembling voice. 'You are brave Sharrie, it is all good. Can you see me?'

'Mmm', I murmured, as I took a short breath.

'Good, good. I'll be right back, okay?', He said, his voice now sounding steadier and rushed out of the room.

An old, grey haired man, probably a doctor of some kind, arrived shortly afterwards. He entered the room slowly, followed by Bob, who looked as if he was totally out of breath.

'Good morning, Miss Swift. How are you today?' The doctor asked, as he approached the bed, looking down, straight at my irises. Bob sat quiet. I knew he would have wished to confirm that I had indeed just woken up, but he knew the doctor was trying to get me to talk.

I smiled insincerely, disappointed I could not decipher the doctor's blank face.

'Very well, I am Doctor Garcia. Can you look up here?' He said, flashing the ophthalmoscope on my left iris. 'Look at the light please. Last night you gave us a really hard time, Miss Swift. We almost lost you.'

I blinked in surprise. I wasn't expecting him to be that blunt with a patient. Undisturbed with my reaction, he focused the light on the right eye for another second. Then he turned the instrument off and gave me a thoughtful, compassionate look.

'But you have the heart of a lion, you should be thankful for that.'

I smiled again. I could not stand people who pitied me. It made them feel superior.

'Now, you will need to rest for two more days. For now, your condition is stable, there is no imminent risk. Do you remember how many painkillers you took?'

I shook my head.

'Okay, do you remember what medicine you took?'

I shook my head again. His voice turned business like, the sympathy gone.

'What do you remember from last night?'

'Mmm, the last thing I remember is that I lay down in bed after I had taken some…' I paused and put my head down as I couldn't bear the idea of Bob listening. 'Then, I don't recall anything. It is all blurry.'

'All right, no problem, it is normal not to remember what happened afterwards. It is due to trauma. You will soon remember more, but one step at a time. First, your body needs to build up some strength. The pills have not caused damage to any of your vital organs, and your stomach has been fully cleaned up. As I said, your body fought very hard last night.'

He exchanged a look with Bob, who seemed to have heard that before.

'We will continue to monitor your condition for two more days. Then, hopefully, you will be able to go home for Christmas. You may even be able to eat a bit of turkey.' He smiled and opened a folder he had been holding under his arm. As he put his eyes down, he muttered slowly. 'But I warn you, Miss Swift, you have to get some serious medical help this time, and I don't mean for your body... You swallowed a dozen painkillers last night. You were lucky to have been brought here on time. Had you arrived an hour later; your brother would be arranging your funeral right now.'

Bob looked down; his face contorted instantly. Having noticed his distraught face, the doctor continued, this time with a cold, patronizing tone, 'I have never come across such a devoted, brave young man. You are lucky to have such a brother, Miss Swift. Now, we will perform a few more tests in the afternoon. I will come at 6:00 p.m. Try to get some rest and not to think too much.'

I nodded but he was busy scribbling in his file and completely ignored me. Bob followed him out of the room and returned a few minutes later with a light, relieved smile.

'He sounds just like grandma.' He said, after closing the door behind him. I smiled back, astonished by his ability to break the ice like that.

'Yes, he does. He seems to like you though.' I murmured, suddenly feeling pain in my stomach.

'Yeah, old pervert.' Bob smirked and placed a chair beside my bed.

'Funny.' I said and took a short breath, fully aware that his joke had been an attempt to make me feel easy. 'How did you get here? I placed my hand on my tummy, as if trying to figure out where the pain was coming from.

'I took a direct flight.' He smiled and leant over me, taking my hand into his. 'Get some rest Sharrie, we will talk later.'

Bob was studying at college in Boston, to become a mechanical engineer. I thought that it must have taken him a good seven-hour flight to get to London from Boston. God, I could still not believe he had made it so promptly.

'Does mom know?' I asked, still confused.

'No, no one knows. Don't worry.' He said quietly, still holding my hand firmly.

I sighed. It was such a relief that mom was unaware of what had happened. I hadn't planned to see her reaction. In fact, I had not planned anything. I was surely guarded by some fierce angel to be able to stand next to my brother, who was zealously trying to act as if nothing was wrong. Or, perhaps I was really dead. Maybe that was death, a different dimension altogether, where I could build up hospital rooms, grey haired doctors and the spitting image of my brother. How could I know for sure? No one knew what death was like. It was all too easy, I thought. One minute I was gone, the other I was back in the game.

'How did I get here?' I asked, tired of my heavy thoughts.

Bob looked down, as if weighing up how to best respond. 'Your neighbor Lucy heard you last night. She and her friends knocked down the door… and then… then they drove you to the hospital. She contacted me and asked if she should tell anyone else. I asked her not to so I am the only one who knows. Mom doesn't know, no one knows.'

I sighed again. 'Ok, that's good, I will try to get some sleep.'

'Yes, you need to rest. I will be right here.'

Bob pulled the blanket up to my chin and moved the chair back to the end of the room, by the bright window. I closed my eyes and tried to sleep, somehow feeling happy that this time around I would be able to wake up.

London, 24 December 2017

Bob had insisted on renting a new apartment, so I had not argued with him. Probably, it was better that way; I wasn't yet ready to lie down on my old bed. Sins and sorrows from the past would dance around my head like nightmarish ghosts.

We left the hospital on Christmas Eve and drove straight to the new place, an old Victorian building, set in a popular, historic area.

The one-bedroom apartment was on the second floor, overlooking a commercial café that seemed busy with young people. The surrounding felt like a replica of my old place, a busy street with loud people.

Bob had tried hard to choose a flat in the midst of noise, hoping that crowds could help make me feel a bit less lonely. He had however missed to realize that the problem wasn't the feeling of loneliness, but rather the lack of it. I did not need comfort from hundreds of moving mannequins, roaring around the house to feel better; I had plenty of noise in my mind. All I needed was peace and sanity.

Bob had picked up some of my belongings from the old flat. He had spread them neatly around the new apartment; my books lying in straight rows on the living room shelves; the work laptop on the small desk by the bed and the shoes in the hall wardrobe.

Once in the bedroom, I lied down on the new, king size bed. I was too tired to glance around, but I could feel on my face the bright sunlight, slipping gently through the window curtains. The pillows smelled of chlorine, or maybe it was the floor. I wasn't sure, but that feeling of chlorine cleanliness and warmth from the sun felt like a God blessed christening. I felt reborn; tired and weak, but light and serene, in such a way that only life after death could be.

The following day, before waking up, I knew it was Christmas day. The unmistaken buttery smell of a Christmas cake sailed through the apartment like a breeze of love at first sight. Since early morning, Bob had been trying his hands at baking. He had also brought an enormous turkey and was working to deliver an exquisite roast. A tiny, Christmas tree, decorated with golden baubles, was melancholically looking at me from the living room.

I got the impression that Bob was trying to persuade me to get up. I lay in bed most of the day, but I could hear noises from the other room, dishes moving around, plates clacking and a blender roaring.

It was funny how history repeated itself, time after time, as if it was running out of new ideas. I had deja vus of that exact same scene, years back, when mother cooked the exact same dishes and decorated the tree with the exact same colors.

During dinner, I sat down at the kitchen table opposite him and tasted a bit of cake. I knew I could not eat a lot, as I had been advised to follow a strict diet for the following two weeks. Nevertheless, those few bites were the most pleasant in a long time. They tasted like childhood and happiness. I wanted to congratulate him for his cooking skills, but the words would not slip out of my mouth. I hesitated because the Christmas dinner was a trap; a Trojan horse, placed in front of me as a seduction gift. If I accepted it, I was bound to pay a price, the price of sharing my story.

The truth is, I strongly believed that sharing my stories with others meant that in the end there could be only one version of events. And I wasn't ready for that. I wanted to be able to twist the events how it suited me, depending on my mood. In my euphoric days, I wanted to be able to dream of changing myself, as much as I wanted to drown deep down the ocean, in my nights of misery. I wanted to be free to punish and pardon myself. That is why I never liked talking to therapists either. They always tried to translate me. For each word or action of mine, they tried to find a name, a sound word to describe it. And then, they tried to fit it all in a story, with a beginning and an end. But they failed to see that words and actions did not define me as a whole. I was all those words and actions and at the same time I was none of it. With myself, on the contrary, I could talk for hours; I could turn the tables every time I felt desperate or lost. I could be a winner when I was a loser, and I could choose to be a loser when I was a winner. I was the owner of my destiny, the only one able to tell my story…

I knew Bob was expecting me to begin a conversation; he gave me quick, curious looks time after time. He had probably rehearsed in his mind what he was going to say during dinner. God, I felt like a death row prisoner eating his last, favorite meal, while the officer beside him anticipated in anguish, a final opportunity for confession.

Bob broke the silence muttering something with his mouth full.

'The turkey is good, isn't it?'

'Hmm, yeah?' I said, my head still stuck on the death row prisoner meal.

'Yes. I put some cumin and oregano in it, like mom does. Try it.' He said, keeping his eyes on the turkey.

'I noticed that, I will try it now. The cake is great, by the way.' I said and tried some more cake.

'I thought you weren't here when you were chewing that cake. Was your head back in Great Falls Town?'

'No, not really. I was just thinking you have spoiled it with too much sugar.

'Hah, you are quick to retaliate, huh?' He smiled and sipped some water. 'Now Sharron, what do you think of this flat?'

'It is all right, too many people in the street, though. It might get noisy during weekends.' I complained.

'Yes, you are right. But it is good for a month or so. I have been thinking about this whole situation, you know. I think it is best if you come back home with me in January. You have been running away for too long. It's the best thing for you, for all of us.'

'I am not ready to come back. I need more time.' I said and took a deep breath. He deserved some sort of explanation, I thought. 'Look, overall, I am better off over here. I really am. This whole thing was a momentary snap. I don't know what I was thinking.' I said in a neutral tone, as if nothing big had happened.

'It wasn't a snap. It wouldn't have happened this time of the year, if it were. You had planned it. And you know it.' He paused, put the fork on the plate and glazed right through my eyes, as if reading my thoughts. 'I think you should come with me. I don't know what you're doing here, anyways.'

'I am not coming home. It would only get worse. You should go back to college in January and forget about all this.' I crossed my arms over my chest and turned my head to the side to avoid his withering look. 'I'll seek medical care. I'll sort myself out this time.'

'Oh yes? Why should I believe you? You have been fooling us for some time now, with your stories of perfect, big city life. You have misled us into thinking you have a successful career and a happy love life. None of that is true... You will come to Boston with me. We can share an apartment together in the university campus. This will be temporarily of course, until you get better.'

I stopped for a second to take a deep breath and then gave him a brutal, hateful look.

'Do you think moving to a new place will actually help me? How? You don't get it, do you? I am empty, empty inside, hollow, skeleton and flesh on the outside only. You can't invent happiness by throwing in a new city, house, job or friends. Life is more than that.' I pushed the plate towards him and looked away. I imagined Bob would become traumatized by that hostile confession; however, I was disappointed to see that my plan didn't work out. He was used to my extroverted outbursts of anger, which came as often as the death-like introverted silences, so he didn't move a muscle in his face.

'Sharron, I do get you, maybe not what you are going through, but I get you. I get you, when you tell me you feel stuck on a train carriage going to the same old, nasty place. But you need to get off the train at some point, walk out of the station and take a pleasant stroll home. That's what I am suggesting. A little change may help you freshen up.'

'Why is it that we try to solve an old problem by creating a new situation? I said, certain the move to Boston was a bad idea. 'Diversion is no solution; I know this first-hand from the many therapists I have seen. It is cheating your own self. I am staying here, Bob. I need to solve my problems, not divert them.'

'We can talk about it later, after dinner, okay? Have some turkey, please.' He said and pointed with his knife at the turkey.

'No, we are not. This is the only conversation we are having.' I said in a tired voice and chewed some more cake.

'Sharron, this is not the right moment to argue. Don't forget, you know I can make you come home if I want to. Would you like me to talk to mom about all this?'

'Are you threatening me now?' I flipped, and put the cake back on the plate. 'You still think I care, right? Well, not anymore. How can you intimidate someone who would be dead by now, hadn't it been for some random neighbor?'

I did not get an answer from Bob as his phone rang loudly, like the whistle of a boxing referee. He stood up and answered the call, strenuously pretending to sound excited.

Mother was on the other end of the line. I understood he had been telling her that he had paid me a surprise Christmas visit and that we had been sightseeing around London for most of the time. He had seemed credible as she was asking him to get her some mince pie and English tea.

'Hey Sharrie, mom wants to talk to you.' He said with a nervous, distrustful look, as he handed the phone to me.

There was a short silence before I could grip the phone and speak to her. It was ironic to hear my mother talk about our holidays; talk about me in such an incredibly excited way. I had imagined the first conversation I would have with her would have been in spirit form, somewhere in a different universe. I had assumed I would apologize for the pain I had caused her and explain I had finally found peace. Remarkably, the universe had changed the course of my plans, reinforcing an undisputed dictate on the stream of events. Maybe it all happened that way so I could understand how peculiar death and its aftermath were. Or maybe I still had unfinished business in this world.

'Dear, did you cook anything nice for Bob?' She said at some point, with her unmistaken crispy voice. I could hear the words flowing quickly, as if she was multitasking or rushing to finish some house work.

'Kind of, mostly he did though.' I said, ready to burst into tears. 'He's done a great job with the cake; you would love it.' I looked up at the ceiling, hoping to concentrate on what she was actually saying.

'I thought he wanted to work during Christmas. As usual, he changed his mind in the last minute. Why didn't he tell me he was coming over?'

'I don't know, maybe it was a last-minute plan. He might travel to Europe after Christmas.' I lied; my voice now calmer.

'Oh darling, don't encourage him to travel a lot. He has to study for his exams. Maybe it is better he returns to college after Christmas.'

'I know mom... I told him the same.' I walked to the window, to avoid Bob's intent look.

'Great. He needs to be reminded occasionally. You know dear, I am standing in front of a 5-foot tall spruce right now. It is just by the fireplace, where we normally have it. I have tried to decorate it, but haven't managed too well with my weak legs. I ordered it online, they have changed their systems, can't just drop by the shop to get a decent spruce nowadays. John McAlester delivered it here, himself. Bless him, what a kind hearted man. Still working twelve hours a day, just like thirty years ago. He asked me about you, you know.'

'Oh, yes? How is he keeping up?'

'He is all right now dear; touch wood, as long as he takes his medication. He is a hero, few of us manage to get past through cancer like that. You know, Anthony was also here with him. Apparently, he has taken over the family business. Such a lovely young man. You know, he helped me set the spruce by the fireplace. He also asked if you are visiting any time soon. I mentioned you are always travelling with work these days.'

'Good, good, mom. So, Anthony helped you with the tree?'

'Yes, he did. He offered to help me with the garden too. I kindly refused, but he insisted, so I gave him the keys to the back garden. Next weekend, he will come over to do some trimming and weeding. The garden is a mess, dear; I can't keep up with it. I am not able to stand up nowadays; I need to take constant breaks. My knees are giving up on me.'

Since my parents' divorce in 2005, mother had given up on looking after the garden. That had been father's job, so she felt she wanted to leave it all messy, to remind us that things would never be the same without him. It was as if she still hoped for him to come back, even though, he was now living in Texas, married to a woman half his age and almost never visiting us.

'You could have paid someone to do that job. I wouldn't like you to get help from him or anyone else. Please call him and ask for the keys back.' I said, irritated.

'Sharrie, I can't do that.' Mother continued, in her usual, calm voice. 'It would be rude. You know them, they are good people. You should show more respect to them, considering what they have done for you.'

'All right mom, do as you please. But promise me, this is the last time you get any help from him.'

'Very well, I promise. But please dear, can you try and be a bit more positive for your own good? It is Christmas.' She said and took a deep breath.

The rest of the conversation felt like a long, freezing shower, I was numb and longed to get out, but had to wait for my hair to be washed first. Mother was always tactful with me, but couldn't help being patronizing.

After the phone call, Bob sat down, crossed his arms over the chest and mumbled to himself.

'So, Anthony's been visiting mom.'

'Yes, it seems so. I don't understand what he is trying to prove by helping her.' I said, this time looking Bob in the eye. The atmosphere in the room had suddenly become conciliatory. The frosty looks had softened and the tone of our voices had flattened.

'Sharrie, things have changed. It's been a long time. Maybe it is time for you to forgive him and move on.'

'It is easier said than done...'

'Listen, you can't continue to poison your soul with such hate. Not after what happened last week. You need to truly let go if you wish to recover. This level of animosity is eating you. Wouldn't it be better to meet him for a change? This way you could find some peace with yourself. What do you think?'

'I do not hate him. How can you hate someone who's been dead to you? No one can hate the dead; it is human instinct... Simple.

'Sharrie, this is not helping you.'

'By the way, I don't intend to see him or anyone in Great Falls Town, as I have no plans of ever going back to Vermont. But I have come to realize something, these past few days. You see, I spent many years hoping I would someday sit down with Anthony and for that I had prepared a long, confronting monologue with do's and don'ts.

I had rehearsed in my head his reaction, the counter arguments and had even pictured an ending, in fact, several of them. But it all went down the drain. He never came to see me. Maybe, he thought it was better that way. Or maybe, he was scared, scared of the truth, my truth. I had hoped that meeting would have solved some mysteries and helped me get back to my feet. But you can die and still reach no conclusions with people. So, you have to assume you have had that conversation and that you did conclude somewhere. This way you can heal your wounds.'

'Sharrie, you wouldn't be doing these things if you had your wounds healed. You would not give up on us if you had concluded somewhere. How could you do this to us? How could you do this to mom?'

'That was just a snap, Bob. I am sorry for what I put you through. I am glad mom is oblivious. But it is over, I promise. I have learnt my lesson. I will seek good medical care.'

Bob seemed unconvinced. However, he didn't want to ruin the positive flow of the conversation so he continued with a confident tone. 'Listen, let's make a plan. I stay here for another month while you recover, and then you decide if it is best to live here or move to Boston with me. And, as for Anthony, we can just forget about him altogether. What do you think?'

I paused for a moment then nodded with hesitation. 'All right, let's not fight anymore over this.'

Bob raised a smile, a solicitor type of smile, like winning a court case or signing a good settlement deal. He stood up, raised his glass of water and shouted emphatically: 'Very well, old sister. Merry Christmas to you! We shall see you live a long, happy life.'

I chuckled awkwardly, somehow hoping that would not be true. 'Merry Christmas, little man! I will outlive you; you can bet.' I lied.

'Haha, yes, you most certainly will, as long as you don't try to cross the border to the other side. It has happened twice... There won't be someone to save you a third time.' He winked and sat down, grasping joyfully the cutlery from his plate.

'Oh yes, thanks for reminding me.' I said, pretending to be annoyed.

Anthony had saved my life once, I thought, but only so that I would try to take it ever since. Maybe he wasn't meant to, after all.

Great Falls Town, 02 December 2007

I could not tell how long I had been like that. All I could feel was Christie's long, soft hair hanging over my face, her salty tears sliding down my lips as she spoke to me. 'He's saved you, Sharrie, you'll be all right. Hold on, we are almost there.' Her words echoed through my ears like megaphones: 'He's saved you; he's saved you'. I could not understand for what reason someone had to save me; I was in no physical pain after all. But, at the same time, I had no recollection of what had happened. It was as if someone had reformatted my mind. I was trying to think, to remember. My thoughts were blank though, to the point I had to give up trying.

Despite the memory blackout, my senses were quite dynamic. There were people around me; I could tell by their loud, authoritative voices. I could also distinguish the roar of a straining car engine in the background. It was rattling and whirring loudly as if it was in pain.

Judging from the speed of the car, I assumed I was being taken somewhere, most likely to a hospital. The thought did not frighten me; on the contrary, I felt safe having Christie near me. I could sense that someone, a medic perhaps, was doing something with my neck. He had grasped my neck tightly and was pressing against my forehead with force. I wanted to see Christie, to tell her I was okay, so I forced my eyelids to open, until a faint glimmer of light slipped in. It was then that I noted Christie's forehead. It looked bright red, as if she was wearing a Santa Claus hat. It must have been due to shock, but after seeing her like that my eyelids sagged down and my senses muted, until it all went dead silent.

Great Falls Town, 04 December 2007

Bob was carelessly playing with a toy train on the floor, a step from my bed. The jarring sound of the train carriage had woken me, but his adorable little figure was too perfect, so I had not dared to disturb him. Instead, I stood there silent, looking at him as he spoke to his train.

He noticed me somehow and ran furiously outside shouting: 'Sharrie is awaaaake!' A few seconds later, mother and grandmother appeared on the door, clearly breathless. They had been taking coffee from the machine which was just a few steps down my room.

'Hi mum.' I whispered, reaching for her hand as she approached slowly. She stared at me for a second and then suddenly burst into tears, dropping the plastic cup of coffee on the floor. Grandmother bent down to fetch the cup and little Bobby, who had been hiding behind her, stood there numbed, his eyes ready to explode in tears.

'Hi sweetheart, how are you feeling?' Grandma finally asked.

'I'm okay. What happened?' I asked, a little puzzled.

'You had a small accident, sweetie. But nothing serious, you will be discharged in a few days.'

'Yes honey, you will be fine. Don't worry about the arm, it's a fracture, it is not broken.' Mother intervened, as I began to scan my body for scars.

'And this, what's this?' I asked, terrified, looking at the rigid neck brace.

'It is for your neck, honey. You hit your head in the accident. The doctor said they will remove it in a week or so, right?' She looked at grandma for further assurance. Grandma nodded insincerely.

'I don't remember a thing... How did it happen?' I asked again, more confused than scared.

'You were going to get the spruce with Christie and her father and there was snow on the road... and the car slid... It slid on the snow.'

'How are they? How is Christie?'

'They are all right dear, both of them. I will ring Vince now.' She said in a weak, trembling voice and picked up the phone.

I knew mother did not quite like Mr. Jones. It wasn't due to Christie's long hours of work at the restaurant; no, on the contrary, she praised him for showing her that money did not exactly grow on trees.

In our small town, it was common for teenagers to assist their parents in their businesses after school, and Christie was no exception to that. The truth is, mother disliked him for something a lot more personal.

She despised the stubbornly small and orthodox window, through which he viewed the world. Mother, who worked as a biologist in a small pharmaceutical firm that had recently been established in a neighboring town, had travelled around when she was younger. She always encouraged Bobby and me to move out of Great Falls Town, when we finished high school. Mr. Jones, on the contrary, had never been out of Great Falls Town, so his take on life was somewhat different from hers. According to mother, the indifference Mr. Jones was showing towards Christie's higher education or future career prospects away from Great Falls Town came as a direct result of his shortsighted worldview. He did not quite understand how big the world was and what opportunities lay ahead out there, she said.

I generally agreed with her, but what I didn't quite understand, was her hesitation to ever confront him with her opinion about Christie's future. She never argued with him, or even advised him to encourage Christie to study more. She said it was not worth trying to change his mind, and blamed it all on his upbringing.

Even though, she was technically correct about Mr. Jones, she was not really being honest. Like most people in Great Falls Town, mother was a conformist. She knew that most children would inherit their parents' businesses - such things had been ongoing for generations, so she didn't want to be the one to challenge the status quo... Even for someone like Christie, she felt she had no right to intervene.

These small differences aside, mother and Mr. Jones, in general, got on very well. They had a lot more things to unite them than divide them. They were both single parents, raising their children on their own, so they understood each other's struggles pretty well. Mother often said that she respected Mr. Jones for raising Christie to be a hardworking, fine, young girl, who spent all her limited, free time doing charity work at the church, rather than hanging out with friends. That gave me particular joy, because it seemed to me that mother had really captured Christie's essence, her big, loving heart and compassionate character.

Christie came to the hospital a few hours after mother had called Mr. Jones. She jumped to my bed like a rabbit and gave me a long hug.

'Hey sleeping beauty, I missed you.' She said, her pink cheeks popping up as she smiled at me.

'Hi you, what's that on your forehead?' I asked tediously.

'It's nothing babes, it's just a scratch.' She said and touched lightly the white dressing on her forehead.

I tried to push myself upright to see her wound better.

'Sharrie, please don't move.' She yelled and looked towards my mother, who had started to march to my bed after noting my sudden moves.'

'Why not?' I asked curiously.

'You need to get better, honey.' Mother said. 'Your head is a bit fragile.'

'I am well, mom. Mr. Jones... how is he?' I asked, pretending to not have taken notice of the 'fragile head' comment.

'He is okay; he's broken his right arm, just like you. At least his head is in its place, Christie said, pointing at my neck brace.

Mother's jaw dropped and her eyes widened with shock. She smacked her lower lip and moved closer to my bed, as if to shield me from Christie's poisonous remarks.

I did not pay attention to mother's reaction. I laughed strenuously, because what Christie had just said was actually quite funny. Christie knew I needed a bit of sunshine in that moment, a bit of normality. And I loved her for that. In her presence, even the most serious of accidents seemed like every day events. Nothing in life was to be taken too seriously. Not death, not even life itself. I lacked that optimistic vibe which so much seemed to define her.

Hiding behind Christie was little Bob who had also been smiling at her joke. Mother had noticed his smile and had given him an icy, patronizing look. Bob's face had instantly re-contoured to shout out guilt.

'Hey Bobby, your old sister loves to sleep. She's had us all waiting for her to wake up, just like sleeping beauty, right?' Christie said, caressing his soft, fine hair. Bob did not smile this time.

He opted for a safe, sad look. 'She has been waiting for a prince to wake her up, right?' Christie continued, looking guiltily at my mother who refused to have eye contact with her.

'Yes, I am the prince.' Bob said timidly, grasping my hand with his little fingers.

We all laughed. Mother nodded in agreement and gave Christie a conciliating look. Bob had successfully managed to melt away the tension between them. As Christie began to say something to Bob, someone knocked on the door, so she paused and turned around. Two men, dressed in heavy clothes, as if working outside in the snow emerged, the older one holding a bouquet of fresh flowers. Initially, I thought they had come to the wrong room, but after watching mother's warm welcoming words and gestures, I realized they had come to see me.

They greeted mother courteously as they walked inside, and handed her the flowers. The old man apologized for his wife not being able to join them. Mother thanked them both a few times before walking slowly towards me.

She went on to introduce them, constantly shifting her look between Christie and myself. The men were John McAlester and his son Anthony

McAlester. They smiled as they came closer to me. It was a pitiful smile, I could tell. For some strange reason they felt sorry for me.

Mother chatted with them for a while as I remained silent and slightly confused. To break the ice, she told them I had some difficulty remembering things, which was normal, considering the impact on the head. She then turned to me and explained that Mr. McAlester and his son had helped in the accident and we, as family, were very grateful to them and would be so for the rest of our lives.

I was still puzzled but nevertheless smiled back and thanked them for coming to see me. I knew John McAlester a little. There were no big secrets in Great Falls Town, and certainly, suffering from a life-threatening disease was not something you could hide. As the rest of the community, I had heard rumors about his long battle with an aggressive tumor. Luckily, he had recently improved and looked more and more healthy.

The McAlesters owned a shop and a small cafe at the top of the hill, which boasted the best scenery of Great Falls Town valley. As kids, we used to go there with the school, each end of term, to celebrate the upcoming holidays.

It was still fresh in my mind how he used to warn us to not walk to the edge of the cliff to take photos. We disliked him for that and secretly called him names. With time, however, I had grown to "forgive" him and rather like him.

Mr. McAlester was an old school type of man, the type who spoke very little and worked very hard. It was difficult to get to know him well as he made little effort to talk to people. He always seemed distracted, busy doing his own things. It was hence no surprise that I didn't really know him that well. I did, however, know his wife Fiona, who came to St. Thomas church every Sunday. She kept her head fully covered in a black mantle and prayed for hours, always sat on the last row, as if to avoid talking to people. She seemed a bit detached, but I liked her, as she always greeted Christie and myself when we met at the church.

We knew what she was going through and did not expect a lot of gentility from her side, however, unlike many other women with similar problems, she always smiled at us. It was a strained smile, but it was enough to make us girls happy. Father George, who knew Mr. McAlester well, had asked us a couple of times to say a prayer for him. I remember repeating the prayer after him, thinking of Mrs. Fiona instead; her black mantel and sad, almost defeated look.

The only member of the McAlester family I knew almost nothing about was Anthony. I had heard from mother that he left town to study, when he was a teenager. It was strange in a small town like ours - where people knew everything about everyone - to remain under the radar like that. I, for starters, had never seen him before. I estimated he would be in his late twenties or early thirties. Around six feet tall, blonde, with very short, soldier-like hair and a well built, robust body, he was easily noticeable. His eyes were dark blue and resonated warmth which contrasted with his husky figure and deep, low pitched voice.

Anthony looked different from us. It was either the clothes or the mannerisms; I wasn't sure, but he was definitely different from us. I was curious to know how he had helped in the accident, as I did not recall a thing. Had I met him before, I would certainly remember. He was too good looking after all.

'You keeping up, soldier?' Mr. John McAlester said, as he sat on the chair by the bed.

I nodded lightly.

'I knew it, you and I are fighters! We fight till the end. We never give up. These eyes have seen a lot of things, but never ever a braver girl. Do you hear me, child? Never, ever give up. Even when the world is against you or the odds are not with you. Never give up on yourself.' He said, his eyes pinned on mine, as if trying to unleash any doubts I could have about my willpower.

I smiled, throwing a brief, worried look at Christie. She lowered her head and avoided to have eye contact with me. The tone of the conversation felt very deep; it had suddenly changed the atmosphere in the room. A bizarre silence followed after that, as if a plot had been uncovered. I knew mother would never tell me, had I been very ill, but Christie would. I knew she would; we had no secrets. Even if I were to die, she would tell me.

That is what best friends did. They always told each other the truth, no matter what. Now, I was starting to feel angry with Christie, with mother and grandma too, even with little Bobby. They had set up this little theatre stage with sleeping beauties and charming princes to distract me. They had doped me into believing I was all right. But all of a sudden that didn't seem to be the case. Was John McAlester right? Did I have to fight against the world, even when the odds were against me? What did he mean by that? I surely deserved an explanation; it was my life at the end of the day.

I could sense a growing fear rise inside me, the sort of fear that starts slowly from the stomach and then builds itself up around the ears, eyes and mouth, until you can't breathe, hear or see anymore. I knew that wasn't the right time to ask any perplexing questions, so I tried to remain calm and raise a faint smile instead. Thank God for Anthony McAlester, I did not need to smile for too long. He quickly intervened and effortlessly turned to Christie.

'And you Christiane, are you feeling better?' He said, as he sat down on the chair besides his father.

Christie nodded with hesitation.

'I saw your father yesterday morning, as I was driving past the restaurant. He was busy cleaning the snow off the pavement. How is he?

'He is a lot better now, thank you.' Christie said as she raised her head up.

Anthony, judging by my puzzled expression, thought it useful to give me an insight on what his father and him were doing there.

'Sharron, my father and I happened to be at the accident scene... Like the rest of the folks there, we did our bit to help, until the ambulance and the firetruck arrived... But, thank God, you seem to be getting better, right?' Anthony's voice dropped as he gave me half a smile.

'Yes, I feel better now.' I said and exchanged a brief look with him. He looked sideways, glancing initially at the floor and then up at my mother, who remained stubbornly static, like a Greek marble statue.

'How did you help? I mean, in the accident, how did you help?' I asked, as I stared at him.

Anthony McAlester sighed lightly and turned towards his father who also looked uneasy.

'Well, we were driving down the hill and saw the car... The ambulance and police arrived shortly after the incident, so the three of you were taken straight to the hospital. We didn't really do a lot to help. Your mother is very kind... Anyone would have done the same... Anyone.... You guys were lucky.'

'I don't remember it.' I said, upset with myself for not being able to recall a thing. Not remembering was equal to not living, my grandma used to say. The idea that entire blocks of memories could be turned upside down, vanished or mixed up gave me a powerless sensation, as if I had no control over my life. And the sad thing was, I did not know how to fight it. I just had to wait for those tiny patches of time to be sewn in together, until the full mosaic could come back to life.

'Honey, the doctor said the memory loss is temporary only. You will start to remember things bit by bit. Just give it some time. We are all here for you. There is no need for you to upset yourself. I mean, apart from the accident, you do remember everything. Isn't it, Christie?' Mother suddenly spoke up, finally emerging from the lethargic shock. Christie nodded in agreement.

'It is due to the impact. You will soon be okay, soldier. Just don't worry about it.' John McAlester said firmly.

Anthony McAlester smiled at me, as his father continued to talk. As I stood there silent, I noticed that he had a soft face, which was well hidden under his military posture and muscle-bound built. I was glad he had come to see me. In the back of my mind I knew that soon after he left, I would need to have a serious conversation with mother about my condition. But for the moment, I was just glad to have him around and enjoy his company.

London, January 2018

As advised by doctors, I recovered slowly in the following days, to the point where, by the end of January, I had no more abdominal pain. Throughout this time, Bob stood stoically by me; he became my nurse, my cook, my friend and family. Each week, he accompanied me to the doctor appointments and took notes on what I ought to eat and what to avoid. He remained intensely serious when he spoke to consultants and watched carefully every word they said. Then he asked questions, many of them, particularly about future side effects. At home, he would repeat the doctor's advice until he was pretty confident, I remembered all the instructions.

What I loved most about Bobby was his determination to uplift my mood. He made weekly plans and wrote them on a calendar which he had pinned on the kitchen wall where I could clearly see it. Part of the schedule was a short daily stroll along the river, which got longer and longer as the days passed. Initially, I had been reluctant to engage in such activity, scared I would be compelled to talk about myself. But surprisingly, we never talked about me. In fact, we spoke of everything else but me.

We gossiped about old neighbors and school teachers. We talked about father, grandma, cousins, my work and everything else in the world. If that had been a strategy of his, I did not know, but it was certainly working well. I did end up looking forward to the daily strolls. I felt rejuvenated each time I returned home and even set myself up for some cooking and reading in the evenings.

Bob was aware of my love for science fiction films, so he had set Friday to be our day for a movie night out. We usually went to watch extraterrestrial fiction movies or time travel thrillers.

On our way back home, we discussed the ending twists, the characters and storylines. I became chattier as the days passed and felt a lot more optimistic. Maybe unconsciously I hoped for a chance to start over again. But deep down, I dreaded the day Bob would have to leave, as I knew I could not pull it off without him. I usually kept these fears to myself, but as the days passed and January drew to an end, I realized something needed to be done.

One afternoon, when we had just returned from our daily river walk, I sat down at the kitchen table and told him I was ready to relocate to Boston. Bob was initially at a loss for words but then walked quietly to the fridge and with his face hidden behind the door muttered with half a voice. 'Why did you change your mind?'

'Because I am scared.' I confessed. 'I am scared I will do it again. And I don't want to. But I will. Because I think about it all the time. Over and over again, I keep thinking about how to do it, how to end it. And I really want to get myself distracted, but it just doesn't work. Nothing really works. I can't fix myself, I can't redeem myself, no matter what I do. I am a total failure.'

'Sharrie, please. Stop it, please. You are not a failure.' He said in a weak voice that looked like an honest protest.

'You know I am. But I have seen what it's like on the other side. It is very lonely and painful. There is no tunnel of light, surrounded by white angels that greet you tenderly. In fact, there are no angels whatsoever. There is no redemption. Just pain and the stink of figs.'

'I know sis, I know. But it is over. It won't happen again.'

'I want a second chance, Bob. I really do. But there are times at night when I feel there is no point in trying. I think to myself: What will I resolve by staying here? What will I change? Nothing. I had my chances and I failed. Maybe the world is a better place without me. But then, in the morning, I watch you make my favorite cup of coffee and I feel as if I deserve a second chance. This veil of ambivalence is lifted away and I become a new person. I would like to feel like this all the time. To feel there is hope.'

'You will, Sharrie. I promise you. I promise you; the future is all yours. This time we will sort it all out. Now, let's celebrate your relocation!'

Bob sat down and opened a bottle of champagne that he had brought back from the fridge. I only took a sip, as I wasn't yet allowed to have alcohol. When I finished it, I felt I should never get back to drinking again.

We spend a few hours chatting, and I felt more positive than I had been in a long time.

Who would have imagined, little Bobby who cried each time I left him home to go out with friends, would be the one and only I could turn to, when I needed the most? My little brother, my greatest hero.

London, February 2018

I returned to work on Monday, the third of February, after more than a month of leave. I was lucky enough the department was small and only had to report to Reza, who would not mind me taking a month of unpaid leave, as long as the HR department did not ask any questions. We were four in total: a part time Finite Element analyst, a project secretary, Reza and I. They were all lovely; quiet and discrete, which was ideal for someone like me that struggled to make up stories about a family incident type of leave.

It was early in the morning, when I arrived at the office. The sky was grey outside, but I tried to remain positive. I had struggled to picture myself sitting again at my old, lonely desk. But I knew that it would not continue for too long. I had decided to hand in my notice that day, which meant I had to only work for four to five weeks before I could pack for Boston.

I entered the building from the main entrance door, the one I had been avoiding since I had first joined the company. The desks I passed by on the ground floor were mostly empty but that didn't stop me from keeping my head high up. I smiled randomly at people as I walked through the engineering department quarter and noticed they smiled back at me. Some wished me a Happy New Year, which I felt was quite nice. Some even asked if I had been on a long holiday back home, and I, pleasantly surprised, struggled to cook up a believable excuse.

I had never thought someone at work would have noticed my absence, but inexplicably, some of them had. I continued with a quick, confident pace towards the geotechnical department quarter, quietly thinking to myself: 'Well begun is half done'. However, three feet away from my desk, the confidence wall, I so much had struggled to build, fell apart.

It broke down into tiny pieces that instantly gathered to form a gruesome anxiety fence around me. I sat quietly on the chair and watched in horror a malicious scene unfold itself before me. Scattered around the desk, like beheaded revolutionaries, were my old, faceless friends. Their black and yellow stripes had been damaged, their leads and erasers cut off.

Why did people have to do that? Why did they have to hurt them like that? Simply because they could not scream and hurt them back, simply because they looked invisible? Sometimes, you can serve someone your whole life, yet it is not enough to earn their love, I thought. I picked the pencils carefully and placed them on the top drawer of my desk, thinking I needed to leave that place the soonest I could.

I must have stayed numb for a few minutes as my bag was still on my lap when Reza yelled from behind me.

'Hey Sharron, finally here. Good to be back? How are you? How was your trip back home?'

I jumped when I heard my name, and then smiled at him guiltily. 'Hi Reza, I am well, thank you. Did you have a good holiday break yourself?' I said, as I did not really remember all the questions, he had fired at me.

'Yes and no. My mother-in-law was here for New Year, old, grumpy woman. But well, what can I do? Need to keep her happy, otherwise my wife will end up just like her mother.'

I laughed and put my bag on the desk.

'Now, read through the emails to catch up. Nothing has changed; it is still quiet over here. But some work may be coming along. Come to my office at 10:30, will you? I need to show you something.' He said, pointing his index finger to me.

'Yes, sure Reza.'

'Good, good. And, send out an invite for me; I have a meeting at 4:00 p.m.… Ah, please, also check the heating in the meeting room. You know, they never manage to get the temperature right in that room, no matter how many times I complain about it.'

I smiled happily. God, I had just realized I had missed my boss. 'Yes, at four, right? Interview or meeting?'

'Meeting. You don't need to come; it is project budgeting crap.'

'All right, I will send it now.' I said, as I spotted another pencil behind the computer monitor.

Reza disappeared in his office and I turned on the laptop, thinking I needed to get started on my resignation letter.

At 10:30 a.m., I walked into Reza's office, holding a small notebook, where I had inserted a printed copy of the resignation letter.

'Come in, Sharron. Take a seat, please.' He said, with an excessive politeness, as if I were a client or an interviewee.

'Everything all right?' I said, as I sat down on the uncomfortable chair in front of him.

He stood up silently and closed the door behind me. Then he sat on his chair and gave me a hopeless look.

'Yes and no. Look, I will be straight with you, as I have no other options. The company is thinking of closing down the department. They are planning to negotiate the terms of our redundancy packages next month. The process is still in the air, but bottom line is... we will all be laid off. And, I wanted to have a chat with you first, before we start official negotiations... I have not spoken to the others in the department, as I know they are not in a position to help. But you may be...'

I sighed. 'Oh God, wow...That is terrible. How can I help?'

'We don't have enough projects to keep us going, as you know. And most of the bids we have been working on have either been put on hold or... we have lost them to competitors. The only project we have is the "New Millennium", which is being managed by the office in Dubai. Now, they are willing to help us with some work, but they would need a geotechnical engineer to relocate there. They would need someone to collect soil samples from the construction site and investigate the properties, settlement details and so on.

Then, the data will be transferred to the office here and we can generate the soil profile curves and do the necessary analyses and reports. Is it all clear?'

'Yes, I understand. So, you are suggesting I relocate to Dubai?' I asked, suddenly feeling nervous.

'I mean, you have done this type of work in the past, so it should be straightforward. It is just that you have to be there temporarily. Until we win a project. Otherwise, all four of us will be laid off...

'I see. This is awful news.'

'Yes, I am sorry I had to break it like that to you. You haven't yet settled back in from your long holiday, it must be dreadful to hear it. But it has been a dreadful time for me as well... I have not even told my wife about it. It is truly shocking; you spend your entire career with a company and then they are ready to throw you in the street just like that...Anyhow, I wish I were in a position to relocate to Dubai, but I am not. I am too old now. And you are the only other geotechnical engineer here. So, I don't have much selection choice.' He said and put his palms on both cheeks.

I sighed again. 'All right, Reza. Give me a day to think about it. I will come back with an answer tomorrow.' I said nervously, not really knowing what to make of the situation.

'Yes, of course. Take your time. I know it is not an easy decision to make. By the way, do you have someone here, I mean a boyfriend or so? I think you have not really mentioned anyone, right? I do know that your family lives in the States...'

'No, I don't have a boyfriend... But there are other things to consider. I will decide tonight.' I said and bit my lip in an effort to stop myself from speaking.

'Yes, of course, there are other things to consider...In any case, here's a sample expat contract. It will give you a good understanding of what to expect when you get there. The salary stated in the last page is what you will be offered. But, if you are unhappy with any of the terms, let me know…We can always amend a thing or two.

'Okay, I see. Thanks Reza.' I murmured glancing nervously at the contract.

'Thank you, Sharron. Now, please keep this to yourself, I would not like the others to feel panicky about this whole situation. It is not fair to them… to any of us.'

I nodded and walked out of his office; the notebook still clutched under my arm.

I spoke to Bob in the evening and as I had expected, he was unhappy with the idea of relocating to Dubai. His main concern was that I needed to see a therapist and that it would be more difficult to do that on my own, without someone to support me. He believed that my condition, meaning my mind, was still unstable and that could lead to unpredictable actions on my side. I tried to convince him of the opposite. I mentioned that it was better to relocate to a new place; far away from home, where I had no past experiences to affect me. I promised to see a therapist in Dubai and Skype with him every other day. He still remained unconvinced, but did not argue with me.

In the end, we made a plan. I would spend three months in Dubai and if I liked it, I would stay. If I didn't like it there, I would move to Boston.

Great Falls Town, December 2007

After the McAlesters had left the hospital, grandmother took Bob home to rest. Christie left soon afterwards; she had to get back to help Mr. Jones at the restaurant. That night, they were hosting the annual Christmas dinner buffet for the National Society of Veterans. Christie normally served drinks and talked to the guests; however, this time she had to help in the kitchen as one of the twins was off sick. I was upset that she had to leave. More than that, I was upset that she would spend the evening on a beautifully decorated table by the fireplace, under twinkling Christmas lights, while talking to people and enjoying some of Mrs. Elliott's best cakes. I, on the contrary, was stuck in a cold, empty hospital room that smelled of antiseptics, under blinding, white lights that gave me shivers each time they flickered.

Mother was the only one left in the room with me; she was tired, but still kept tidying up – an old habit she had got as a teenager from grandma and had not been able to ever get rid of. Since the McAlesters had left, she had remained silent, hoping that I would not bring up any of their remarks.

At times like that, I felt sorry for mom. She was a single parent, who had to do everything on her own. Dad didn't really care to look after us. After he tied the knot with one of his younger colleagues in Austin, Texas, he would come to Great Falls Town only once or twice a year to spend a few days with us. Even now, that I was admitted to hospital, he had said that he had invited his in-laws over for Christmas and didn't want to upset them by leaving. He had promised to fly over to Great Falls Town the soonest he could, but I knew he would come to see me in April, at his usual timing.

My parents had met at the University of Vermont while studying biology. They got married soon after graduating and then relocated to Great Falls Town, where a large pharmaceutical company had its headquarters. For nearly fifteen years they worked together, developing experimental drugs to fight dementia.

The company struggled financially, and in 2002, they laid off half of their work force, my mother included. Father was asked to relocate for a year to one of the company's smaller offices, in Austin, Texas.

Mother stayed behind in Great Falls Town, to look after us.

By 2004, my father was still working in Austin while the rest of us were in Great Falls Town.

That same year, my parents separated. To put it more bluntly, father dumped mom after she discovered that he had been having an affair with one of his junior staff members. They got divorced soon after. At the time of the divorce, Bob was four and I was twelve.

I grew up looking up to father, and when he left, I resented him. It wasn't bitterness that I felt, it was pure disgust at his lack of accountability.

The divorce was amicable, but that is not to say it wasn't hurtful. Mother suffered for years, even though she never accepted it. That whole ordeal left her with a huge vacuum, which she was unable to fill with anything else.

Father, on the other hand, continued to have a successful professional career and a happy new family. Mother lost both her career and husband, but she got us, Bobby and me. At least, that is what I liked to think.

I watched mother's slim, exhausted figure wandering around the room and decided to not ask any questions.

However, when she finally came over to the bed and started tidying up the overbed table, the nerves won the battle over patience.

'So, mom, what is it exactly that I have?' I fired the question at her, more eager than ever to know the truth.

'What is it, dear?' She said calmly and headed to the other end of the room to pick up Bobby's toys that were lying all over the floor.

'Mom, please don't go away. What was Mr. McAlester saying? What's wrong with me?'

'It is nothing, dear; we just have to wait for all the test results to come through. We are not hiding anything from you.'

'Please... Tell me, what is it they think I have?' I said, almost ready to burst into tears.

Mother turned around and walked back towards me. She sat on the chair by the bed, her eyes heavily swollen by the lack of sleep.

'Okay dear, I want you to listen to me carefully. It is nothing serious, but I want you to be patient till the end. Okay?'

I nodded with some hesitation.

'Well, the thing is... there is a chance of... brain injury, due to the blow on the head. We don't know yet how serious it is. It might be a mild trauma or it could be worse. The signs are you have a mild concussion...'

'What signs?'

'The amnesia and dizziness, the confusion and God knows what else.' She rubbed her hands up and down her jeans and looked away.

'But I don't sound confused, do I?'

'No, not at all dear. But we have to see how you get on in the coming weeks. They say the brain is still reacting to the impact. It might be swelling or there may be tears that can affect its future functioning. The thing is, such tears are difficult to heal. They need time.'

'Oh, I see, this is not it, is it? It might get worse, right?'

'The doctors are positive, honey. You just need to rest. This will take a few months; I mean, the full recovery may take even longer than that. But, let's be positive. The doctors have said the memory will gradually come back. We just have to be patient and do whatever is needed.

'I am sorry, mom, for all this. I am sorry for what I have put you through.' I said tearfully.

Mother stood up and came closer to me. She gripped my hand and held it tight. I noticed the black circles around her eyes had suddenly become more visible; she was not just looking tired; she was now looking old.

'Don't worry, honey, you will soon be okay. One day, all of this will look like a bad dream.' She said and for some strange reason looked up at the ceiling.

The first few days in the hospital were crowded with visitors. From school friends to relatives and neighbors, they all showed up at my hospital bed with sad, miserable looking faces.

I was grateful and pleased to have people around but could barely answer any of their questions, which always revolved around the accident and its repercussions. Soon after they were gone, I was left with a bitter feeling of numbness and self-pity, which I could not stand.

Fortunately for me, there were also pleasant visits, like the ones from Christie or Father George, who managed to brighten my days. It was strange how two diametrically opposite characters had such a tremendous effect on me. Christie's loud, buzzy visits made me want to get out of bed, run outside in frenzy and laugh at the top of my lungs.

Father George's on the other hand prompted me to live and be happy with my own self, my own world, a world I had the luxury to share with no one. Both of them were a healing balm, a silent driving force inside me.

On his last visit to the hospital, Father George asked me to join him at St. Thomas Church for the Christmas buffet he was organizing for Great Fall Town's homeless people.

In the last three years, Christie and I never missed to volunteer at the buffet party. We normally worked on the food section; distributing soup, lasagna, cake and everything else the cooks had prepared for the event. We also made sure that there were always drinks, cutlery, plates and tissues for everyone on the tables.

Different local businesses had supported the dinner buffet for years, so by now it had become an annual tradition in town, a tradition that filled Christie and me with joy.

I promised Father George that I would join him at the church, if I was discharged from hospital by then.

Mother didn't like my response. She reminded Father George that it all depended on what the doctors advised us. I knew however, that there was nothing that could stop me from going to the buffet, especially if Christie would be there.

Other friends and relatives were kind enough to invite mother and me for lunch or dinner at their homes, after I was discharged from hospital, but I really didn't want to go to any of those places. I just wanted things to be as they used to before the accident.

I wanted to get back to my routine, my normal life. And that meant that every morning of my school holidays I could go to Paradise Restaurant and spend the entire day with Christie.

Despite the visits and courteous dinner invitations on my address, the days at the hospital were still very gloomy; I was in pain and felt dizzy most of the time. During such days, strangely, Anthony McAlester came to my mind a lot. I wished he would come to see me again. His father, John McAlester had stopped by instead, this time accompanied by his wife Fiona. Unlike the first visit, this time around he had been a lot quieter, but had still managed to upset my mother with his sanguine hopes of recovery.

Ten days after the accident, I was finally discharged from the hospital. The first days at home were pleasant; the painkillers managed to keep me numb and pain free. It was during the second week that I started to feel pain. Initially it was the migraines, then the instant blows on the head – evil sledgehammers from hell slashing through my brain without mercy. I spent the nights sleepless, wandering around the room like a ghost, exhausted, yet scared to put my head on the pillow.

Mother tried to help; she opened the windows for fresh air every time my head boiled hot and closed them only when I couldn't bear the cold. She replaced all light bulbs in the house with dimmable lamps and covered my bedroom windows with thick, heavy curtains. All noise in the house was kept to a minimum, mother even made Bobby wear headphones when watching his favorite cartoons.

For over a week after I had returned home, Christie had not come to see me. I was upset, as her phone calls had been brief and she had sounded tired and rather detached. I wondered if I had said or done something, but I struggled to recall in detail our conversations at the hospital. I only remembered how she tried to make me laugh by mocking my grandmother, and that was about it. I didn't remember much else. But I was confident I had not done anything to upset her. It must have surely been mother or grandma who had spitted some senseless rubbish around her.

The buffet at St. Thomas church was happening on December 20. Tired and sick of being at home all the time, I had asked mother to call Father George and confirm that I would be going there, but only for a couple of hours. The decision had been a compromise with mother, who initially had refused to drive me there.

I had called Christie a day earlier, to ask if she was going to help at the buffet and she had said she wouldn't be able to, as she had to help at the restaurant, while Mr. Jones was doing a check-up at the hospital for his broken arm.

Slightly disappointed by that, I decided that I would still go to the buffet. After all, I had promised Father George that I would be there.

The church of St. Thomas, which Christie and I had attended since we were children, was the oldest protestant church in Great Falls Town. Built in 1924, just before the Great Depression, it was all covered in stone, which was very attractive and different from other buildings in the area. Relatively small for the expanding Great Falls Town's community, with only 150 available seats, the church was not the first choice for large masses. It was however a hot tourist spot, and in the summer, it was always busy with people taking photographs.

The years before the Great Depression were very prosperous and the church reflected that time perfectly. It had a lavish architecture and a classic interior design. It also had a big garden at the back, which was often let out for social gatherings or wedding ceremonies. The later had been Father George's idea, who had a sharp nose to find opportunities and boost the income of the church.

By exploiting such opportunities, Father George had been able to do a lot of charity work in the community and for that was regarded by many as a hero.

These details played in my mind, as I entered the tiny church that was now buzzing with people from all its corners. Upon seeing us, Father George rushed over to greet mother and I. Before I could really say "Hello" to him, he asked if I was ready to get my hands dirty with work.

I nodded happily and followed him into the church. God, it felt so good being given some work! I was tired of constantly being asked about my head, my arms, my neck and my amnesia. Finally, I had met someone with sense!

Mother said she was also happy to help while she was there, however she was quick to point out that we only had an hour to spend at the church. We would need to get back home so that I could take my medication, she said.

Upset with mother, I wanted to refuse her stubbornly stupid decision, but I held my tongue. There was no point bringing Father George into our family arguments, I thought. He was too busy with the buffet and also so very pleased to have us there to be distracted by that nonsense.

Knowing that the hour would fly like a second in a busy place like that, I started to put down the tissues and bottles of water on each table.

In less than ten minutes I was done with my work, and was feeling very proud of what I had just achieved. Mother was still chatting to people at the entrance of the church and I deliberately moved to the far end, so I could get to do some more work, away from her prying eyes.

When I reached the altar, I saw two young men, setting up a ladder, right by a tall, green spruce. A large box, full of Christmas ornaments was on the floor next to the ladder.

Out of curiosity, I approached the box and before lifting my eyes up from the glittery ornaments, a familiar voice sailed through my ears like a warm summer melody.

Anthony McAlester was up two steps on the ladder, when I murmured a shy 'Hi' to him. He was holding a large yellow star that was meant to be put at the top of the spruce, but unfortunately didn't quite make it there, as Anthony came down to greet me back.

'Sharron, what a nice surprise to see you here.' He said in his serious, baritone voice, as he came closer, clearly looking happy. 'You look very well; do you feel better now?'

'Yep, I am *much* better, thanks.' I answered briefly, thinking that he was no different from the other senseless people before him, who had asked the same senseless question over and over again. 'Is the spruce from your father's shop?' I diverted the conversation, hoping to give him a second chance.

'Oh, yes, we thought the tree would look good in here. It will add to the Christmassy atmosphere. What do you think?

'Yes, indeed, it is beautiful. That was very kind of you all. Father George must be pleased.'

'Well, he wasn't quite pleased to have a Christmas tree in the church initially, but after some convincing, he agreed to it. I have too many ornaments here, some of which he has not approved yet. The toy soldiers, for example. He has banned me from using them.'

I laughed when he showed me the tiny red nutcracker soldiers that had been taken out of the box.

'Here you go', Anthony continued, clearly happy to have seen me laugh. 'You can have them. They match with your lovely scarf.' He said and pointed at the red scarf that was covering my neck brace.

'Oh thanks, I will take them.' I said and pursed my lips, a little sad that he had led the conversation to the neck brace.

Anthony, probably realized my mood shift and quickly put the soldiers into a plastic bag and handed it over to me.

'You will soon not need the brace... Anyways, don't worry about it, you still look very pretty.' He said confidently.

I froze for a second, because I didn't know what he meant by that. Anthony, however, wasn't bothered by my reaction and continued to say something, which I didn't quite catch, as mother was now standing right in front of me, talking loudly over Anthony.

We talked a little more with him and then wrapped up the work that was left, before noticing that the hour had passed and we had to drive back home.

Dubai, March 2018

The first thing that struck me, once I got off the plane in Dubai was the sun. It was bright and powerful and made me squint hard. My eyes continued to itch with discomfort all the way until we reached the airport building. Oddly enough, I did not feel upset by the bothersome itching, I felt rather thrilled. Someone had told me that God travelled with the light, and if you could not see the light, you could not see him either. I liked to think I was a rational person, yet I was somehow confident that with that much light in the sky, I would not be able to ever harm myself again.

The taxi driver smiled at me shyly as I exited the arrivals gate, while rushing to get the luggage off my hand. He was old and thin and badly dressed; a bizarre contrast to Dubai's frenzy of consumerism. On the way to the office, he mentioned that from the accent I sounded American and asked where I was from. I said Vermont; almost certain that he had never heard that name before. But, to my surprise, he had. And he had heard about the snow, the forests and the maple syrup too. He had met many Americans in his home country, he said, some of whom had been from Vermont. He told me Vermont's maple syrup was supposed to be the best in the world, even though he had never tried it and we both laughed in disbelief.

As we drove through the city center, he explained that he had settled in Dubai in the early 90s, as a Kurdish refugee. The war had taken his two daughters and his eldest brother. None of them had ever held a gun in their hands, he said, yet they had been shot dead while driving a car through Baghdad's town center.

It was hard to believe him, talking of the war like that, so effortlessly, so unemotionally, like reading a story from a fiction book. It was baffling to me how some people found the strength to deal with their pain patiently, without ever giving away the slightest hint.

Could it be that through all the darkness he had found a beam of light and was holding on to it ever since? Perhaps he had. Perhaps, I thought, someday, I was to find one too.

The car stopped outside the main offices of the company. The taxi driver got out first and placed the luggage at the building entrance door. I followed him slowly, my heart wretched with pain. As he walked back to his car, he waved his hand in the air and wished me good luck. I looked at him as he smiled at me, the tired, wrinkled eyes screaming with pain and did not dare to try and comprehend his suffering. He got in the car slowly and I stood there numb, like a total fool. I wished I had said something back to him but I didn't. I only smiled in anguish and walked towards the building entrance door.

'Hey, you all right there?' Someone behind me muttered and as I turned, I bumped into him.

'Liam! Hi, sorry, I didn't notice you. Were you here somewhere?' I said and took a step back.

'Yes, I was just behind you, having a cigarette. Did you come straight from the airport?'

'I did… You know, the taxi driver who dropped me, did you see him? Is he still there?'

'I saw him drive away a second ago. Did you forget something?

'No, well, I didn't thank him… I mean, I didn't leave a tip.'

'No worries. Do you need help with that?'

I nodded with a distracted smile and let go of the luggage handle.

'You're sure you didn't forget something?' He said with a slightly concerned look and took a quick step forward.

'Yeah, pretty sure.' I muttered guiltily and followed him.

'All right, so, you're all sorted to start work here; apartment, visa, health and safety certificates?

'I believe so. Next week I'll start work on site.' I said as I tried to keep pace with him.

'Very well. You think you'll like it here? There are loads of shopping malls around the office.'

'Yes, it's been lovely so far. There is so much light in the sky. It is always sunny around here, isn't it?' I smiled and lifted my eyes to meet his.

'Wait till you start work on the construction site, it will be unbearable over there.' He said and put his head down.

'But it is still pleasant… The light I mean, is pleasant.' I said in a feeble, discouraged voice.

'Here you go, Sharron. Engineering department is on the second floor. Finish off work with HR on the third floor and come by so I can introduce you to the rest of the team.' He said, as he stopped in front of an elevator. He then paused and stared at me for a second, as If he wanted to say something else. But then he changed his mind and moved off hastily.

The first week in office was quite hectic. I spent most of the time attending induction training courses that would allow me to work on the construction site, and whenever I returned to my desk, I found a pile of documents that needed updating, checking or signing.

We were seven engineers in the department and all of us shared the same area with the operational team, who were always loud and busy. The desks were set in an open floor area, arranged in straight, parallel rows, which meant that everyone could listen to everyone's phone call or conversation. Initially, I found it hard to concentrate amidst the noise and distractions, but by the end of the week I got used to it, to the point that I started to enjoy the constant tumult around me. With all the workload and fuss, there was little time to think about myself, and that in a way was a relief. When I returned home, which was usually in the evening, I felt so tired that I even forgot to text Bob. I crashed on the sofa and went into a full hibernation until the next alarm bell went off.

The second week, I was sent to collect soil samples on site. I began work at 7:00 a.m. and worked a full, twelve-hour shift. Despite the heavy coverall and boots and the long hours of work, I relished my time there. There was too much light in the sky to begin with, which boosted my motivation. And then, there was the construction staff; the ground workers, steel fixers, plumbers, truck drivers, electricians, storemen and all the others who welcomed me with open arms. I was asked to join their daily lunch and tea breaks and gradually became chattier and more amicable towards them. My introvert, stone like personality subsided into a softer, more welcoming persona. Most of the conversations we had during lunch revolved around work, families and the so many countries we all came from. As I sat amongst them, I realized how similar they were to me. They all felt lonely and missed their families. And they all had problems too. Some had unbearable mortgage loans and expenses for their children, some had old parents who needed assistance and some, like me, had health issues. It was strange, but I felt as if those lunch breaks were a lot more efficient than the endless meetings I had been forced to have with therapists, which consisted in abstract, analytical conversations about my state of mind and led to cryptic conclusions, written carefully on their notebooks, as I struggled to pull through. Here, in a smelly canteen, full of dirty, red uniforms, I was made to feel something more than just desolation. I was made to feel I was not alone, that there were others like me. In fact, there were many more like me, who struggled with their own invincible battles. We were all on the same boat, dirty, red coveralls, sharing each other's joy and sadness, compassion and eagerness. We were brothers in arms. We were faceless little pencils.

Working on a construction site would be a daunting and intimidating experience for a woman, I had been told. There were lots of rumors about girls not being taken seriously on site, but to my surprise, I found out that being a girl had its own benefits, and one of them was to be offered assistance without much persistence.

On a normal, routine day, I would collect soil samples in the morning, drive them to the laboratory and then spend the afternoon in the office. There, I would transfer the data logs to the office in London for further analyses and would write site investigation reports.

In the first few weeks at work, I did not see much of Liam Monroe. He was busy rushing off to meetings, walking in his characteristic, quick pace, with eyes focused at some distant point in the room. When I first arrived in the office, I found a desk in a corner of the room, besides another empty desk. I put my stuff there, thinking it was an appropriate place for me, less noisy and more intimate. Liam Monroe's office was at the other end of the room, nearby the elevator. As I normally took the stairs, I did not see much of him during the day. Occasionally, when he happened to be near my desk, he would nod his head lightly and mutter "All right?", before he would continue with his usual business.

I liked Liam Monroe. As a manager, he was direct and honest and had a "we'll make it work" attitude, which I thought was very positive and uplifting for the team. On a personal level, he was a bit frigid though, at least as far as I was concerned. He never spoke to me for more than five minutes and when he did, it was always work related. Whenever I happened to see him in the kitchen, he was always busy chatting to other people and made little effort to engage me in their conversation. And when I rarely tried to make small talk, he never had the courtesy to speak to me or look me in the eye. Luckily, there were always people around who made the effort to stretch those moments of chatter to a minute or so. That said, each time I had a work-related problem or query, he would pop by my desk and spend a good half hour or more to resolve it. That was perhaps the thing I liked most about him, the flair for problem solving and resolution. As for the rest, I was happy to stay away from his friends' zone. At the end of the day, we were two very different people, one with a set plan in life and the other still figuring out if it was worth having one. None of us would miss a lot by not talking to the other, so I didn't mind him keeping a distance. In fact, there were days when I even tried to justify him.

I thought that I would have done the same had someone asked me bizarre questions about Marilyn Monroe's death or my life aspirations in our first encounter. The truth is, I was too busy working, to give him or anyone too much thought, at least during weekdays.

As for the weekends, they were a completely different story altogether. They were quiet and dispirited and sometimes even hideous. I dreaded to lie down on my bed, scared that at some point during the night, I would sleepwalk to the balcony or the cupboard, where I kept the kitchen utensils. I stored no medicine or alcohol in the apartment and always left the lights on at night. To lift myself up, and above all, to keep my mind busy, I spent some time at work during weekends. There, I would go through emails and reports, sipping calmly my warm, instant coffee, as the radio music played in the background. After work, I would go for long strolls on the soft, sandy beach and sit on a bench, breathing in slowly the light from the sky. Occasionally, I would take random pictures for mother, who was very excited for my new adventure in Dubai. In the evenings, I would try to cook something and then talk to Bob for an hour or so. He always listened patiently as I spoke of the work on site, the new friends, the long soil test hours and the chaotic atmosphere in the office.

Since I had started work on the construction yard, he had begun to sound less worried about me. His daily texts were reduced to four or five and he did not get himself up at night to call and check on me.

However, his constant plea to find a therapist had not gone away. He continued to send phone numbers and addresses of psychiatrists and even called some of their offices to check if they had treated similar patients. I found the idea of a therapist totally pointless, but I did not argue with him, as it was part of the agreement to relocate to Dubai.

One Saturday evening though, Bob became very hostile; his pale, sinless face turned flaming red with rage, so I decided to take action and settle the issue once and for all. I went to the office early in the morning the following day and started to scroll through different psychiatric clinics. As I was writing down the address of a clinic nearby my home, I noticed the building security guard walk out of the elevator and head towards me. I greeted him as he passed by my desk and then continued to write in my notebook.

A minute later, I heard him wander around the back of the room loudly, opening and closing office doors, and as I tried to turn the volume of the radio up, I felt a light tap on my shoulder. I jumped in horror, spilling the coffee all over the desk, on the keyboard and floor. I sat there petrified, scared to turn my head around.

Someone muttered something behind me and upon recognizing his voice, the panic started to melt. My blurry eyes watched him rush to the kitchen as I stood there frozen, unable to move from my seat. His figure became clearer when he returned. I could see his face was plagued by guilt, his eyebrows frown with worry.

'Sorry about that, Sharron. I didn't mean to scare you.' Liam apologized in a weak voice, as he handed half the tissues, he had brought from the kitchen to me.

'It's okay, the keyboard is still working.' I said and locked the computer with haste, as he began to wipe the files and folders on my desk. Liam pretended to not have heard my comment and continued to mop in silence, seemingly concentrated on his task.

Knowing him, I was beginning to think that he had most likely seen what was on my computer screen. Now he was puzzled and needed some time to digest the news. Maybe he was even feeling guilty for not having been nicer to me in the past. It was common for people to change after realizing I had mental health issues. They became mellow, almost compassionate. I remembered that once, in university, a professor had given me a low grade on a homework assignment. I had become upset and complained to mother about it. The following week my grade had been amended and the professor had become peculiarly supportive, in an almost sympathetic way. Perplexed by his change of heart, one late afternoon, after a seminar class, I had decided to face him. He admitted to having received a phone call from my mother, explaining "my situation". I did not talk to mother for a month after that and never returned to his class again.

Liam, who had probably made up his mind by then on a way forward with me, decided to speak up.

'Sharron, why do you keep all these pencils on your desk? You don't need all ten of them, do you?' He said with a soft, yet accusatory tone, as he was wiping the pencils one by one with a paper tissue.

'No, I suppose I don't need all of them… all eight of them.' I said in a feeble voice.

'Well then, better put them in the drawer. The operations guys are savages, they will find a way to snatch them off your desk.' He smirked and looked me straight in the eye.

'All right, I will put them away.' I said hesitantly and opened the top drawer of my desk.

'Very well... Now, what do you say I make you a good espresso? I have learnt to use the coffee machine since you first showed me.'

'Okay, sure.' I smiled, pleased he had brought up something nice about me but at the same time downhearted by his sudden niceness. I had no more doubts; he had seen the list of psychiatric clinics on my computer screen.

'Let's go then. The espresso you are about to drink is a lot better than this instant junk I spilled all over the floor. I might have just done you a favor.' He sneered lightly and pointed at the dark brown patch of coffee on the carpet.

I wanted to say that it had been my fault; that I had spilled the coffee, but I didn't want to spoil his effort to sound funny, so I nodded in return and followed him into the kitchen.

'You are very busy with work? I noticed you spend many hours on site during the week.' He said, as we walked in the kitchen, pushing his shoulders straight back, his voice now business like.

'Yes... I am trying to get my head around things here. I normally do some report writing during weekends, but it is only for now. I will try to manage it all during weekdays. Just trying to not fall behind...'

He nervously tucked the capsule on the espresso machine and turned his head towards me, staring for a few seconds at my face. 'Very well. If we get busier, we might get someone to help you, especially with the tests. I would prefer you had an assistant on site, so you can concentrate more on the reports and correspondence with London. Can you hand me the milk, please?' 'Yes, sure.' I rushed to the fridge and handed him the milk, once again happy he had remembered I had my coffee with milk.

'Here you are, real coffee, you will not miss that instant junk, I can bet on that.' He handed me the mug and as I gripped it, I noticed his hand shaking lightly. 'I popped in the office today to get some files for the Monday morning meeting with the client. I was thinking to grab some lunch at the burger place around the corner. Did you have lunch?'

'No... not yet.'

'Would you like to come? It is quite hot outside, but it is only a five-minute walk.' He threw me a brief, straight look and then turned towards the kitchen window.

'It is okay, I don't mind walking in the sun. I like the light.'

'I thought so.' He said and smiled cunningly, starring down at his espresso coffee mug.

Great Falls Town, 22 December 2007

On the tenth day at home, a chilly Saturday morning, I asked mother to take me to Mr. Jones' restaurant. I was by then sick and tired of my bed, the endless hours without sleep that had turned the days into nights and the nights into a limbo. Mother hesitated initially, but in the end agreed to give me a ride.

One of the twins had spotted us parking outside the restaurant, and in the blink of an eye, the other twin, Mr. Jones and Mrs. Elliott had flocked outside like happy geese. They gathered around me to form a circle and squeezed me with hugs and kisses. I watched that cacophony of voices, as they all spoke in unison; and realized how much they all meant to me. They were my family, my home too.

Mr. Jones rushed us inside the restaurant, and guided mother to his favorite table, the one by the window, overlooking the lake.

We sat there chatting for about an hour, as we enjoyed some of Mrs. Elliott's freshly baked cakes. Mr. Jones, who shared the same sense of humor as Christie, joked that people were leaving more tips after seeing him with a broken arm. He suggested I came to the restaurant more often, that way tips would double. We all laughed after that, but in his rapidly flickering look, I could sense a dense shadow of anxiety.

Mr. Jones kept looking at my fractured arm, then back at my neck, then again at my arm and so on, scanning me, praying in silence that I was all right. His apprehension became more noticeable when he spoke to mother. He avoided to look her in the eye and sighed lightly, each time he had to say something to her. I felt sorry for all that had happened. I wished I could fix it all, not for myself, for him.

Mr. Jones explained that Christie had stayed at home, as she had been having migraines, but I wasn't sure he was telling the truth.

I knew Christie had a wound dressing on her forehead, which meant she would have experienced an impact on her head. But she never really talked about it. And when she did, she only referred to the wound as a scratch. She had also missed the buffet two days ago, which was quite unlike her. I was now convinced that her wound was much more than a scratch.

We stayed for half an hour more, then headed back home. At the first roundabout, I asked mother to take a turn towards Christie's house.

Christie and Mr. Jones lived in an old, two-story house; a twenty-minute drive from the town center. Mother dropped me outside the front gate and drove off to find a parking place. I had asked her to return in two hours, but she had refused to leave me alone. Mother could be very stubborn when she wanted, especially when she had a good reason. I had not bothered to argue with her, but I was upset, so I walked straight to the back-garden door. This way, I could spend some time alone with Christie.

I heard the loud TV noise as I turned towards the back of the house. At that point, Lisa, the family dog, started barking loudly. God, I thought to myself, this dog is so vigilant.

Even though I was a regular visitor at Christie's house, Lisa, a lovely black and brown beagle, would always bark when I got there. I often used to bring some dog treats for her, so now she wanted to make sure she was getting her food.

I continued to walk, feeling slightly guilty that I had completely forgotten about Lisa. This time it was going to be just me, unfortunately, I thought, as I promised to myself to make up for it the next time I met up with Christie.

As I stepped sloppily on the tight walkway, right up against the kitchen window, I got a glimpse of somebody; blue jeans, no shirt, sipping calmly his coffee, as he stood in front of the TV. Numb as I was, I squinted to see him better. He moved lightly, turned his head to the side and sipped some more coffee. I didn't stir. When he turned his head back to the TV, I crept slowly back, towards the wall. I remained still for a second, my hand raised to my mouth, my eyes wide open with shock.

I inched away to the front gate, my heart pounding faster, my full body shaking. When I finally got out, I ran madly down the stairs leading to the main road sidewalk, leaping down two to three steps at a time, thunderstruck, lost for words.

Mother was crossing the road when I reached the sidewalk. I walked hurriedly towards her, trying to look cool, and asked to be taken back home, as I wasn't feeling well. Mother looked stunned; she put her arm around mine and walked me to the car.

Christie came over to see me that evening. She leant over and kissed me on the cheek, as I sat quiet on the half dark room, hunched on the bed, my back against a pile of pillows. She looked more serious than usual, but still calm. I noticed the wound dressing was not on her forehead anymore.

'Your mom told me about the light.' She said as she glanced over the lamps. 'Is it bothering you a lot?'

'A little… but it's all right like this.' I said and swallowed down a lump in my throat.

'Remember what my grandma used to say, when we refused to play in the garden because we wanted to watch TV instead? God travels with the light, if you can't see it, it means he can't see you either…' She smiled and put her bag on the chair. 'You came over to the restaurant today… Sorry, I was at home… You should have ringed me.'

'Yeah, I should have.' I said, as I bit my lower lip, not quite sure what her grandma's proverb actually meant.

'I didn't feel like working today. Anyways, how are you? Mrs. Elliott said you wiped out your cake, it seems you haven't lost your appetite for cakes.' She tried to put on a smile but it didn't work out, she looked rather odd instead.

I remained stern. Christie came closer and sat on the bed.

'So, when are you due for the next scan?' She asked hesitantly, staring at me.

'All right, cut it off now.' I said, giving her a blistering, disdainful look. 'I saw him today… I came over to the house to surprise you and saw him in the kitchen… What on earth are you doing, Christie? Are you out of your fucking mind?'

She remained still for a moment, then stood up and turned her back on me.

'I know you did. He told me that you saw him. Well, he didn't turn around on purpose; he didn't want to upset you. He wanted this done properly. He wanted me to tell you first.'

'What? Are you insane? Nothing of what is going on between you two is proper. I can't believe you are supporting him like this. Is this some kind of twisted Stockholm syndrome you are suffering from?

Christie crossed her arms on her chest defensively and turned around to face me.

'Wow, wow, chill out Sharrie. First, don't get upset. I don't want you distressed by what's happened. You are more important to me than any of this.' She said and folded her hands in a prayer mode. She had suddenly turned into the patronizing, sophisticated lady, her wannabe alter ego.

'Are you blind? Don't you see this is not about me? It is about you, you fool. He is abusing you. You are only fifteen.'

'In two months, I'll be sixteen. In Vermont, I can get married by then.' She said coldly.

'God, you are missing the point.' I yelled, annoyed at her. 'You are too young to be sleeping with him. That creepy devil is using you, your innocence, your stupidity. You need to grow up first and then sleep with whoever the heck you want.'

'He is not using me. He has talked about getting married to me.'

'Wow, you really think he is going to marry you? Wake up, Christie! You are a teenager. You think he wants to marry a silly teenager? No, no one wants to marry silly, young girls. They only want to sleep with them.'

'Ok, calm down now, please, for your own sake.' She said, in a soft, begging tone. 'Say we break up, so what? So, what, Sharrie? What will happen? I'll return to my daily job. I will work on the till; I will wash the dishes and serve the food. Do you think anyone ever asked me if I wanted to do that instead? While you were camping or doing piano or French lessons, I had to be working full time. Get on my skin... I am living someone else's life. I would not want to continue to do this, if I had a choice. And now I have.'

There was a death like silence in the room. She put her head down to hide the teary eyes.

'This is so wrong, Christie. I thought you loved that place. What's wrong with you? I don't recognize you anymore.' I protested. I was so confused, all the jokes and laughs, the cakes and hot chocolates at the restaurant; they had all been a sham, a bubble. 'Christie, you can't punish yourself for your struggles.' I finally said, this time despaired, my voice sticking on my throat. 'You have to rise above them and become better. That's what we've been dreaming of since we were little girls. We wanted to build on our dreams. Tell me, isn't it what you still hope for? Don't you still want to get out of here?'

'No, not anymore. You should understand, there is more to my life than that silly restaurant. And dad will never let me get out of there, anyways. So, you see, it all makes sense now, right?'

'No, it doesn't.' I flipped. 'It doesn't justify any of this. You should stop this. That monster is manipulating you; he is putting all these gloomy ideas into your head, isn't it?'

'I better leave now; this is not good for your health.' She said and wiped her face. 'I'll come back in a few days… Just try to get your eyes used to the light; you'll need to get out of this bloody room one day. And get rid of these stupid curtains…'

She opened the door and without saying another word, walked away. I felt like a complete fool.

Dubai, March 2018

The sun was bright when Liam and I left the office building. Its warmth together with the delicate spring breeze flying timidly on my face brought on a serene aura upon me, which made me feel less anxious of walking alongside Liam.

The fast food place around the office block was called "Grand Burger". It was a cozy, American style burger bar with a 1960s retro décor, which looked very colorful and slightly hippy. The walls were bright orange, with fragments of John Lennon songs and Indie graphic designs. I thought it was a great choice, at least as far as the décor was concerned.

We both ordered the same top-secret recipe burger, which the "Grand Burger" was most famous for. Liam did not talk much while eating; I guessed he did not want to intimidate me any further. He had probably realized his behavior at the office had been slightly bizarre; unusually friendly, almost fraternal towards me. Now he had decided to sit back and relax for a while. Or at least, he had wanted to make some room for me, to relax alongside him.

'How do you find Dubai?' I finally asked; when we were almost finished with food.

'Well, work wise it is challenging and messy, but it is interesting too. There are lots of things to learn…' He smiled and looked at me, happy I had finally asked something. Then, playing with his knife and fork on the empty plate, he took a shallow breath and continued. 'But, on a personal level… well, I suppose it is not a secret anymore; there are no secrets in this office, anyways… The truth is, my ex- fiancée left me before moving here. She didn't want to relocate over here. So, I have mixed feelings about this whole adventure. But it is all getting better, which is a good sign.' He said and sucked in his lips as if he did not believe his own words.

'I'm sorry to hear that. It must have been horrible.'

'Don't be, it is for the best. Every cloud has a silver lining, they say.' He sighed lightly and looked around for the waitress.

'That's how you manage to remain positive...' I said and smiled at him.

'Yes, we have to always remain positive, Sharron. That's the secret to a good life. That's what keeps the life going.'

'Funny you say that. I know someone who repeats that line every single day. Only that, they refer to love instead...'

'Good, that makes two of us then. For me, it's the sparkle inside of us that keeps the life going.' He said in a euphoric tone and waved at the waitress, at the other end of the room. 'What about you, what keeps you going?'

'Hmm, I don't really know. There isn't much sparkle out there for me, I suppose... I just go with the flow.'

'Well, I don't wake up in the morning thinking I have a mission to save the world either. None of that rubbish. But I see it this way: I work with a lot of people, if I am miserable, then it will affect them, their families too. So, it just becomes a vicious, toxic circle. I don't just do it for myself, but for the others too; for the guys in the office and the workers on site. You have to understand something; it is not always about us, what we do here... It is not just about us. The sparkle inside is for the others around us too.'

'But, don't you find it consuming to always have high expectations of yourself? I know for a fact that I am no superhero material. Maybe I wasn't made to make a difference, or maybe..., I was tested and failed at some point. Now, I would just like to carry on living with it. The world can keep going even with less sparkle, right? There are already too many supermen out there.' I smiled and folded my hands, feeling proud of my confession.

It actually felt awkwardly good to speak to him like that. I somehow wallowed in punishing him with my bitter words. If he wanted to play the sympathetic therapist, he was going to get the mad patient, I thought. Liam didn't seem impressed of my confession, though. He moved back on his chair and gave me a long, mind reading look.

'That is not really true. You moved to Dubai to save the jobs of your colleagues in London. And, from what I see, you are working really hard to help them. The guys on site... they really like you. You work long hours and help, whenever they need assistance. This should be enough to keep you going. Motivation will grow into you, as long as you still care for them. Remember, no one ever wakes up in the morning thinking they will save the world. Unless you are a superman or superwoman, of course.'

He grinned and I, instinctively, did the same. I realized then, on that tiny fraction of the second, when our laughs were synchronized, that there was something about that man. I was feeling something strange; something good. It wasn't just a feeling of remorse for my bitter words. It wasn't admiration or lust either. It was a feeling of warmth, like being wrapped up in a warm blanket, during a frosty winter night. It felt like home, like the buttery flavors of the Christmas cakes we had as children.

The waitress finally arrived and hurriedly placed the bill on the table. Before paying, Liam, who was still looking happy, asked her about the secret burger recipe sauce. He guessed it was barbeque mixed with honey. The waitress shook her head, let down by the answer. She then leant over, and with a smile larger than her mouth whispered to him: 'It is figs sir, not honey, fresh figs'.

Great Falls Town, 24 December 2007

On the morning of Christmas Eve, grandma and little Bobby sat on the carpet by the fireplace, under the fluffy, piney scented branches of the spruce and blissfully wrapped Christmas gifts.

Each time they finished off with a parcel, Bobby would stick a hand written tag with the person's name on it. Then, he would run to my room and show me the parcel, before carefully placing it on a stack of presents at the side of the tree.

That year, Bob had wanted the Christmas tree set by the fireplace; he had said the golden baubles looked shinier near the fire. Grandma had helped him position the spruce right at the side of the fireplace, proudly overlooking the dining area of the living room.

The move had of course meant relocating half the furniture in the living room, but grandma had been happy to do it, as long as Bobby was there to help her out. Together they had weaved the twinkling lights around the branches of the tree, hanged the baubles, placed the glittery golden star at the top and stuffed all the snowshoes with candies and chocolate bars.

A few hours before Christmas dinner, they were still blissfully wrapping gifts, while on the kitchen next door mother tormented herself cooking for us.

In our house, Christmas dinner was equal to organizing a wedding. Mother would get up at dawn to place the cumin and oregano marinated turkey in the low heated oven. Then, she would prepare the Russian salad, the mashed potatoes and the crispy spinach pie, all of which had been old family traditions, and had never missed the Christmas dinner table. In the end, she would bake Bobby's favorite dessert; the snowman shaped biscuits, a special treat for his good behavior throughout the year.

Christie had promised to bring over a peanut butter cake, one of Mrs. Elliott's specialties for the Christmas dinner, so apart from the biscuits, mother had not attempted to prepare any other desserts, afraid that Mrs. Elliott's cake would outshine hers.

A day before Christmas Eve, Christie had called and asked mother to spend Christmas Eve with us. Mother had insisted that Mr. Jones also join us for dinner, but he had found an unconvincing excuse and opted out.

Mr. Jones was a shy man. He would not have endured two long hours in the company of inquisitive and patronizing women, the likes of grandma and mother. He had, however, promised to drop Christie at our place by 6:00 p.m. and pick her up in the evening.

It was the first time Mr. Jones and Christie would not celebrate Christmas together, and I wasn't happy about it. It further reinforced my opinion, that Mr. Jones felt somehow guilty for the accident and desperately tried to make up for it. By all odds, Christie's phone call had been his idea; Christie would have never wanted to leave him alone during Christmas Eve.

She would dread to picture her father eating dinner by himself, in that old, empty house of theirs, while we laughed and danced elsewhere.

What bugged me the most was the fact that Mr. Jones behaved as if I were the only one devastated by the accident, the only one who needed comfort or some sort of compensation. He failed to realize that we had all lost bits of ourselves that horrific day; he had lost his glee; I, my memories and Christie, worst of all, her aspirations. We all needed to stick to our loved ones and I felt that Christie's place, that particular day, was at her home rather than mine.

I had begged mother to call Christie and ask her to stay with her father, but she had said no, noting that we couldn't refuse a guest for Christmas dinner. I knew mother would not have called her, but I had to try. The truth was, I wasn't even sure I wanted to celebrate Christmas with Christie.

I would be too upset to not spill the beans in front of everyone at the dinner table. I was still very angry; and meeting her up in a happy and sparkly environment would only make matters worse. Since I had faced her about the affair, she had not come to see me, nor had she called or texted me. She hadn't even sent any of the twins to deliver freshly baked cakes, as she had done since I had been discharged from the hospital. It was her way of retaliating against me, against my bitter words.

The last time I had met her, I had called him a demon. No, I hadn't called him a demon, I was pretty sure; I had just called him the devil, which he was. In fact, he was a devilish poisonous snake, which had managed to creep into her brain like a disease, and plagued her with his venom, that amalgam of hate and pretentious love, which for the best part was pure hate. That was that, but still, I missed her like hell. I wanted to talk to her, to reason with her.

I knew that if we sat down and talked, she would understand; she would realize that her twisted, new relationship was from all angles wrong. How could she possibly think that devil loved her? He wouldn't have planted so much hate on her, if he did. He only cared for his ego, nothing more. If I explained to Christie the struggles that Mr. Jones had gone through to raise her on his own, she would comprehend that there was no real reason to rebel against her father like that.

We were very young; we had all our lives ahead of us to rebel against more important causes than our silly parents, who were full of faults and bad habits, and who chose to love us in their own, complicated ways, but all the same, deeply and unconditionally.

I had listed all these things in my mind and was ready to convey it all to Christie when she would come to see me. Now that Mr. Jones' car was rattling in our driveway and mother's gushes of laughter got louder, I somehow lost the plot. I couldn't remember the points I had listed, which point came first and how I would go about starting the conversation with her. I felt the breath stumbling in my chest, my heart hammering loudly. I heard their footsteps getting closer to me and felt crippled, lost for words.

Mother entered the room joyous, followed timidly by Mr. Jones and Christie, who did not seem to share the same level of excitement with her. Mr. Jones, who had never been to our house before, took a quick, shy glimpse around the room before moving closer to me. His eyes flickered from the thick curtains to the pile of pillows on my back and then stopped at the old lamp next to the bed, covered with a thick towel. He pursed his lips in discontent, lowered his eyes to the floor and murmured anemically something to me, his voice catching in his throat. I responded back, acting as if nothing was wrong, but he didn't stir. His eyes stood clamped on the floor, his face pale. Mother, who had grasped by then his shock, suggested they left us girls on our own, and invited him to join grandma and her for a cup of tea in the kitchen. Mr. Jones nodded in agreement and shadowed her silently, dragging painfully the door behind him. Christie's eyes followed his bewildered moves anxiously until he vanished behind the door.

When we were finally alone, Christie, who had not said a word since she had entered the room, took off her shoes hastily, grabbed one of my pillows and placed it at the other end of the bed. She then jumped in the bed lazily and pulled the quilt away from me up to her chin.

I reacted slowly, pulling the quilt back, until it covered my mouth and kept it there with both hands. We were now face to face, like we used to be whenever she slept at my place.

She raised a silly smirk and kicked my leg, hoping to get me to laugh, but I didn't move. Instead, I decided to punish her by bringing up Mr. Jones.

'Your dad seemed totally lost; I suppose, you haven't told him anything about my issues with the light?' I said coldly.

Her face turned blank; the smirk gone. 'No, I haven't. I didn't think he needed to know... He's gone through a lot lately... He blames himself for the accident, you know...' She said and revealed her arms from below the quilt.

'How come you feel sorry for him? I thought you hated your dad. That's what you said last time, right?' I muttered; my face half hidden under the quilt.

'No, that's not exactly what I said.' She corrected me, with a towing emphasis on the word "exactly". 'But he is by all means, square and out of date... Actually, sometimes, he reminds me of those ultra conservative, religious fanatics we see on TV. He is not necessarily a religious fanatic, but all the same a fanatic. You know what I mean...' She folded her hands on her chest and with her eyes clamped down on them gave out a deep sigh.

Christie often complained about Mr. Jones being old fashioned and controlling. The truth was, he was far from the feminist type of dad one would dream of, but still, I thought, it was unfair to label him as a fanatic.

'Oh, right? That's why you decided to whore around, to teach him a lesson?' I erupted, and pushed the quilt off my face. My shaky arms emerged from below the burning quilt.

'Why are you so upset, anyways?' She deflected the conversation, just like I had anticipated, using the old ladylike, accusatory tone. 'Most girls have boyfriends at our age. Are you upset because I kept it a secret from you?' She pulled back the quilt and straightened up her body. 'I was going to tell you, but you were unwell. The doctor said no shocks or distress...'

'You know very well it is not about that.' I interrupted her and pushed my body up. 'It is about you, you idiot.'

'Sharrie, it is just a fling, most girls at school have flings. Daisy, Laura, Sue, they are all dating guys from school.'

'No, no one is sleeping with them, like you are. At least be honest about that.'

'How do you know? Anyways, this thing is just to distract myself from the work at the restaurant. It's no big deal, really.'

'You are such a bad liar. Last time, you said that dirty devil was going to marry you apparently. And you were going to live happily ever after.' I said, the blunt irony striking through my words like bullets.

'Don't talk about him like that. You don't know him.' She paused and turned her head sideways, her face looking frigid. 'Anyways, since when do you remember conversations in such detail? You only remember what suits you...' She groaned and bit her lower lip.

'What? What are you saying? You think I am faking all this?' I jumped.

'No, silly, calm down, you just don't remember the important stuff.' She pushed herself up, bending towards me, frontal, ready for fight. 'If you knew, you wouldn't talk about him like that.'

'Oh, yes, I would. You want to downplay what he's done to you, don't you? He's totally got you under his thumb. What's so special about him that's made you lose your mind, Christie?'

'How about saving your life, for starters? Anthony saved you; he literally brought you back from the dead.' She pointed her index finger at me like her grandma used to, whenever she scolded us. Her light brown eyes were now on fire, stifling mine without mercy. She cared for him, I thought, astonishingly, she truly did. She cared for him more than I ever thought she was capable of.

'I know.' I said effortlessly. I didn't want to give her wings by praising him, even though it meant I had to sound rude and ungrateful. That devil did not deserve my sympathy, not then, not ever. 'My mom mentioned that he helped at the accident, when he came to visit in the hospital with his father. I am keeping a diary, you see, I write down what happens every day, in case I forget.' I said, my voice now matter of fact.

'Yeah, right. You know nothing... Do you remember the fire, Sharrie? The suffocating smoke around you?'

'No... not really.'

'Well, try a bit harder. Don't you remember how he got in the car, under the burning flames, and got you out of there? You were trapped inside. You would have died, if it wasn't for him... He risked his life to save you... No one was coming near the car, Sharrie; people were scared it would all blow off. You don't remember the burning smell? You were supposed to be good at smelling things, weren't you?'

I paused for a moment, spinning in my head possible scenarios of how it could have all happened. My mind was however blank, unresponsive to my imagination.

'I don't remember the smell.' I said eventually. 'Only the music, I remember bits of music playing on the radio.'

She remained silent. Her face screamed despair. I wanted in that instant to leap forward and hug her. I wanted to cling to her and cry behind her shoulders. God, why couldn't things go back to how they used to be a month ago? Why had the world turned upside down, all of a sudden?

We both remained silent for a while; I didn't dare to say another word. Christie finally picked herself up and continued with her confession:

'Look Sharrie, I am not like you. I don't have a bright future ahead of me, away from this little, lock-up town. I know; you always wanted me to aspire high, to dream that I could change the world. But things are what they are and I am who I am. I can't change that; I can't change my family. Besides, I have to look after the restaurant and dad eventually. And... as for Anthony, I know... the thing between us is wrong. I know he is much older and that what we have will probably not continue for long. But I don't want to stop it. At least, not now... He makes me feel different, uncommon, you know. He cares for me.'

'For God's sake Christie, this is so wrong, he is only using you.'

'No, he isn't. He is a good person, Sharrie... You know what? I know, at heart you feel the same. You liked him too the first time you saw him, didn't you? I saw the sparkle in your eyes. You got him right, just like I did...'

'Christie, you are out of your fucking mind.' I shouted. 'I am fifteen, of course I am going to like some hot hero walking in the hospital room, bragging he helped save my life. But I won't let him screw me, just because I like him. You understand the difference, don't you?'

'Yes, I do, what I don't understand is your blind hostility towards him. If I didn't know you well, I would have thought there is a hint of jealousy in your behavior. But well, don't worry too much about him. In ten years, we will be laughing at these silly quarrels we are having. And, who knows what will happen to that guy? I might not even remember him.' She said and put both hands on her cheeks.

Before I could say something back, mother had opened the door and was now striding across the room with an excited, quick step. It seemed she had enjoyed the conversation with Mr. Jones in the kitchen. Now that he had left, she had come to us, happy to emit some of the good energy vibes she had gathered by talking to him.

'Right girls, all ready to try some succulent turkey for dinner?' She said, smiling and rubbed her hands.

I looked at her, embarrassed, knowing what Christie was thinking at that moment.

'Yes great, I will give you a hand in the kitchen.' Christie said and pulled the quilt off her legs.

'Honey, you will be joining us, yes?' Mother asked hesitantly, the smile still fixed on her face. God, I thought she was so awkward at times.

'Yeah, coming in a bit. Have you dimmed the lights in the living room?' I asked, and pursed my lips.

'Yes honey, Bob's done that. He is so eager to know what Christie's bought him for Christmas. He knows all our gifts, you see, he wraps them all by himself.' She said, looking at Christie.

'Oh God, so what happened to Santa and all that? Has he all figured it out by now? I tell you what, he'll have to wait this time. He can open my gift only after dinner. This will have to be done properly, for once. That little man is running the house like he is in charge.'

Mother laughed hard and nodded in agreement. She then glanced at me one last time and took a step towards the door. Christie followed her, relieved to be leaving the room.

As mother closed the door behind her, I felt the buttery smell of the cake fly through the room like a homing pigeon, delivering a long-awaited love letter. I stretched my legs to the side and pushed the quilt aside. At last, I thought, something to look forward to.

Christie was setting up the table when I arrived in the living room. Mother was still in the kitchen; I could tell by the plates and cutlery clacking in the distance. Bobby and grandma were sitting on the carpet, in front of the TV. Bobby was showing her how to play a car racing game on his PlayStation.

I sat at the dinner table and watched as they all buzzed around the room like happy bees. When they finally gathered around the table and grandma raised the first toast, all the distress I had been through the past few weeks seemed like a distant dream. For the first time after the accident, I felt blessed to be alive. I thanked God for being able to share that evening with the people I loved. Even Christie's thing with Anthony, suddenly looked like small trouble. She was here, by my side, safe and sound, happy as ever. That's what mattered. In a few years, we would think of Anthony and laugh. He would be some old, torn sock, lost in one of life's many dirty laundries, just as Christie had said.

My instincts were right to feel hyper joyful that night. Soon after, the world would collapse on itself, trapping us all under its rubble. That evening, I was having the last supper, the last, best moment of my life.

Dubai, July 2018

Liam Monroe had become friendlier with me since our lunch together at the "Grand Burger" place. He smiled more often, and occasionally, when I happened to see him in the kitchen, asked how my weekend had been. I didn't have much to say, so I would stand there thinking for a minute or so, until I would recall something worth mentioning. He would listen silently, always patient, always smiling. I suspected he was aware of my introvert nature by then and tried to give me some space.

I did my best to sound carefree though, and once in a while, managed to throw out a couple of questions at him. He answered them briefly, but every time tried to shift the focus of attention to me.

It was clear to me by then that Liam had a crush on me. I felt it each time his eyes channeled through the room to reach for me, each time he softened his voice when I was near him or when he sighed lightly before asking me a question. I couldn't tell if it was affection or affinity, or both, but for one thing I was sure, it wasn't pity. Knowing that gave me particular joy. In the past, I had suffered from an abundance of sympathy, to the point where I felt no one could ever love me before feeling sorry for me first.

Despite the turmoil my life was in, I had started to like him as well. In the beginning, it was pure admiration. Then, it was something that felt more like respect. In the end, I was convinced it was neither. It was love, or at least my version of love, a skinny type of affection that took the chill off my heart, however consuming and tense the love summer rays were at times.

By the end of June, the "New Millennium" project had expanded to the point that there were now two building construction sites up and running. That meant the office had doubled in size, and everywhere I turned, there were people and there was noise. It was a real mess.

Liam was trying hard to sail through the waves of chaos. He was running from one meeting to another, and when he wasn't, he was locked in his office, working through progress reports and presentations. There were days when I didn't get a tiny glimpse of him. I could only see a clumsy shadow behind his office glass door and hear fragments of his imposing voice. It saddened me to see him like that; caged in a room, surrounded by papers and angry voices coming from his telephone loudspeaker. But then I consoled myself thinking that he had brought that to himself, with his high aspirations of making a difference to the world. So now, he had to bear the consequences of having to steer the ship through the stormy waves.

The days when I didn't see Liam were lonely, but not sad. Partly that was because I knew he was only a few steps away from me, and I could smell his fresh cologne outside his office. The main reason, however, was Amir.

As I had been promised, in May 2018, three months after I landed in Dubai, the project allocated an assistant engineer to help me with the increasing workload on site. They offered a graduate civil engineer, who had done similar soil tests at university. Around twenty-one, Amir was the youngest engineer in our team. It was his first ever job.

Amir didn't really have a sense of time. Be it day or night, he would answer emails, order materials or process test results. He would be one of the first to get in the office in the morning and the last to leave in the evening. He would struggle by himself for hours to find a solution, before shyly asking for help.

When Amir first came to the office, Liam had asked me to pack my stuff and move to a seat near the rest of the engineering team. He had pointed at a desk nearby a window, a few feet away from his office, and asked Amir to take the desk on my right. I had agreed hesitantly, knowing I would suffer in the midst of loud voices. However, despite the hubbub, with Amir sat next to me, the days at the office became a little more pleasant. Together, we would have a quick, morning coffee in the kitchen and then do some paperwork, before heading to the construction site.

There, alongside other red coveralls, under the burning summer sun, we would perform all the in-situ soil tests. In the afternoon, after a twelve-hour shift, we would drive back to the office and send the results to the London team.

As the days passed, I grew to like Amir. The reason for that was his athletic, slim figure, which reminded me of Bob, but also the retrieved character, similar to mine. Liam had made me Amir's mentor, a corporate term for someone who looks after a junior engineer. It was the first time I would mentor someone, and in a way, I was terrified. I felt responsible for him; not just for his learning but also for his inner wellbeing. I told myself I had to remain positive at work, even on my bleak days. The funny thing was, Amir ended up helping me more than I ever helped him.

With him, the tests were completed sooner, the deadlines were never missed and I smiled more often. For over a month after he had joined the company, I had thought of harming myself only two times and that too only reluctantly. At last, I was starting to feel proud of myself.

In the early morning of July 25, we set off for the building site with Amir, when I noticed I had forgotten the construction site entrance badge in the office. I dropped him at the entrance gate and drove back.

The sun was boiling hot outside and I was sweating when I entered the office building. I walked past Liam's office, where I smelled his fresh cologne and sat at my desk. It was unusually quiet, the operations guys were all on site, and the few engineers there had not yet woken up to buzz with noise.

I found the badge under a folder, where I had thought I had left it. I gripped it and moved hastily to the kitchen, hoping to get myself a cold glass of water.

I recognized Liam's voice as I walked past the wall that divided the kitchen from the main corridor. It sounded husky and a bit aggressive - his usual tone. I quickly ran my fingers through my hair to get it in shape and accelerated my pace. Then, as I was about to take the last step to the kitchen, I overheard Amir's name. I stopped and listened. Liam was praising him - which instinctively raised a smile on my face, a smile of pride. The others were on the same wavelength with Liam.

They in turn spoke highly of Amir, emphasizing how smart and humble he was. In the end, someone, who I thought was the visiting Health and Safety manager from London, Max Tinwell, mentioned that

Amir's high performance was because he was receiving proper training from his mentor. The others agreed, they complained how they were too busy to mentor graduates, and praised me for making time to guide Amir. I felt butterflies in my chest, as I waited anxiously to hear Liam's voice. He remained silent though. Then, when everyone was finished, his voice pierced steadily through the noise, mumbling something which sounded like "yes, indeed, she's better than I thought..."

Someone from inside the kitchen then jumped over Liam. 'It helps that she is a girl too. He said, in a slightly ironic tone. 'You should see on site, all the workers in line to help her out.'

They all laughed. I took a step backwards, embarrassed. Men will never change, I thought, and turned around to walk away. Then someone else piped up, with a wheezy, thin voice that I couldn't recognize. 'Lads, have you noticed anything off about her though? No really, listen, I'm not joking, she looks a bit weird...' I heard more laughter before the same, nasal voice pitched higher, as if encouraged by the amusement it had caused. 'Now lads, listen, first day in the office, she skulks at the end of the room, out of reach, as if we're going to rape her...'

'You wanted her to sit next to you, old man?' Somebody interrupted him. The others continued to laugh, seemingly enjoying his irony. 'No, listen, listen, there is more.' The man insisted. 'Have you seen the pencils she keeps on her desk? I walked past her once, and I am telling you, she was staring at them. I mean, properly staring at them, as if talking to them. After ten minutes I walked again past her and she was still there, staring at the pencils, man. Now, honest, I am not joking...'

'She is a bit absent minded, that's all,' Liam intervened, his voice now stiffer. 'That's why I have given Amir to her, to keep her on track... It's working, they have both improved.'

'She is slightly unstable. I say she'll not last long here. A few months, at most.' The man with the nasal voice continued. 'There's too much pressure on site for someone like that, she doesn't have the steel for such work. I bet you, she'll mess things up.'

Max Tinwell was quick to break in on the laughs. 'You're scared of losing your job to a young girl, old man? I have seen you stare for hours at those football betting cards. You must be a fucking cuckoo too.'

They all laughed and continued to take the piss out of the man with the thin voice. There was nothing left for me to do but creep away in silence.

I found Amir looking at an AutoCAD drawing when I arrived on site. He was deeply concentrated and didn't pay attention to my numb face. I asked him to pick his instrument and follow me to the spot we had to drill.

It was excessively hot and humid that day. The muddy air was stuck on my skin like glue and each time I breathed, I felt the taste of salty gravel itching my throat. Amir looked drained too. Drops of sweat dripped down his helmet as he tried to set up the cone penetrometer. His palms had become clammy and slippery, and to be able to hold the instrument upright, he had to continuously rub his hands against the coverall.

At 7:10 p.m., an hour after the shift had finished, we collected the data records and equipment and headed back to the East gate. I left Amir there and walked for another eighty yards, to the parking lot. I got the car out and then drove back to him. Amir placed the items in the seats behind and got in the car. I handed him a bottle of water, which he emptied within seconds. We then checked out, just as the site was about to close.

It had been a long day, and I was glad it was over. The conversation I had overheard that morning had been playing in my head all day, like a catchy, new song, where the lyrics muddle up in the head, until it is hard to tell if they come from the song or yourself.

I had been left with a bitter taste of betrayal, combined with sadness and disappointment that had all been stuck in my head like the sticky sweat on my face, and wouldn't let me think clearly. I was so let down that I felt worthless. It was perhaps the first time in a long time that I cared of what others thought of me.

For years and years, I hadn't bothered to fit in the world I lived in. There had never been a sense of ambition or belonging to drive me. I had just wanted to be left alone, in my own little world, with my own little monsters. And then, Liam had convinced me to try and become a better person, to change, to fit in. I had trusted him like a fool; I had thought he meant it when he said I was working well, that I was saving my colleagues' jobs. He didn't mean it. I was never on track; not then, not now. I was an unstable idiot who had fallen for him.

Despite the heavy thoughts throbbing in my head, I managed to keep a stiff upper lip throughout the day. The truth was, I didn't want Amir to realize something was wrong. He had every right to enjoy his job – a job he loved, and I wouldn't tolerate myself to become an obstacle to that.

'Sharron, how did you become an engineer?' Amir suddenly asked and turned the air-conditioning to maximum.

'Oh', I sighed, slightly surprised by the question; the weird song that had been playing in my head all day vanished by then. 'It is a long story. I might tell you some day.'

He remained silent. He was expecting more. 'Well, it's not a very interesting story, anyways. How about you?' I asked, hoping to get him to talk.

'I suppose I didn't like medicine, so I chose engineering. In my family, men usually study one or the other. It's a tradition you know, you are not allowed to fall too far from the tree.'

'I see. I think engineering is a good choice.' I said confidently. 'As long as you like it of course, which you do. Not many people get to work in open air and see the light, the rain or the snow, like we do. And it is mostly about numbers, isn't it? Numbers can't talk or judge. They can be stubborn, yes, but once in place, they are good little friends.'

'Yes, my thoughts exactly. That's why I like what I do. You can comprehend the world so differently, so profoundly, and you don't even need to use words to express it, only a few formulas, isn't it? And you can do so many useful things for the world. And again, you don't need to talk or convince people that your solution is working, because it is there, fact. Most of the time that is... There is of course the office work, where you need to do some talking to get what you want, because the world there is so small, and the people so little. They gossip and bully one another rather than think how to solve problems. I often wonder why some of them are like that.'

'Don't let that get to you. It is such a tiny part of our job.' I smiled and fixed the mirror in front of me. 'Now, I'll drop you at your place, yes? I need to go back to the office to transfer the files to the team in London. They have a couple of hours to work on the material before the office closes.'

'Better drop me at the supermarket, the one close to my flat. I look forward to some ice-cream.' He said and smiled happily. 'So, we need the results for the client meeting on Monday, right?' He added, a little lethargically now, and turned towards the back of the car to get the data logs.

'Yup, we do. I'll have to work on Saturday again.' I said with little enthusiasm.

A second later, Amir was giving me an alarming look. 'Oh God, Sharron, I have left the folder on site. It's not here. I must have forgotten it at the gate. God, I'm so sorry. Please let's go back to check if someone is there.'

'You sure? Did you perhaps put it in the boot?'

'No, I didn't even open it. It's there, I am sure. God, I am so sorry. Please let's go back.'

'All right, no panic. I'll turn around at the next roundabout. Maybe the site is still open.' I said and stepped on the gas.

The East gate was closed when we arrived at the site. The lights were off and the field was dead quiet, resembling a ghost town. The only living soul we found 200 yards from there, at the North Gate, was the security guard, a tiny young man, who was half asleep when we knocked on his window. He spoke nicely, but did not fall for Amir's plea to let us in.

He even refused to go searching for the folder himself. Amir tried several times to persuade him. He made small talk with him to find out common friends and even offered him a cigarette, but none of that worked. The guard, who as it turned out, had been doing the job for only a few days, did not help us. In the end, we gave up. I told Amir there was no point wasting more time and asked him to get in the car. Before turning the engine on, Amir turned around, and with a secretive, gumptious look, a look I had seen before, proposed something radical.

'I know a way in,' He said. 'If it is still open, I'll be back in less than fifteen minutes.'

'What? No, no way. We are not playing James Bond on a Friday evening.'

'Please Sharron, I want to do this. It's my fault, I left it there.'

'Forget about it, I will speak to the clients on Monday, they will understand.'

'Maybe they will, but are you sure our guys will?' He asked in an almost ironic tone and gave me a side eye.

Apparently, the kitchen conversation I had overheard in the morning had not been a one-off event. Idiots, I thought, didn't they have anything better to do than gossip about my state of mind?

I wondered how many times in the past they had been telling stories about me, how many times Liam had called me names. 'She'll mess up, she doesn't have the steel for such work,' kept ringing in my head and I suddenly felt angry with them.

'You know what? Let's do it.' I said to Amir who immediately put on a smile and nodded his head in agreement.

The workers had cut open a section of the fence that surrounded the construction yard. It was at the back of the parking lot, where it was least visible, due to the many cars parked in the area. The teenagers who sold cigarettes and alcohol would enter the site from there. This I learnt from Amir, as we walked around the fence, searching for the open section.

Once we found it, a hole of no more than ten inches, Amir got in first, stretching the fence away from me as I crawled in. I noted his right palm was cut and some blood showed up in his thumb. We continued to walk silently through the parking lot, when halfway through, the lights turned on. Those were human sensor lights, something we had not anticipated. We kept walking. We knew that in ten minutes we would be out of there. Unfortunately, when we reached at the East gate, the young security guard was expecting us with a patrol car parked outside the gate. He had called his mates, and they were all there, with their lights and radios and the loud voices that overshadowed even the loud alarm sirens of their car.

I asked them to not call the police, but rather inform the client office. I mentioned it wouldn't be very nice for the police to know their firm had neglected to see an opening on the surrounding fence. Their contract could be suspended in the best case and there could be worse consequences for all of us involved and for the project progress too. The young security guard rejected to see my point, but luckily, one of his mates, was more accepting. He called the client office. I requested we called our manager, so that the issue could be handled amongst us. He agreed.

Liam Monroe arrived at the construction site sometime after 9:20 p.m. He listened carefully to what I had to say, and asked few questions with a formal yet calm voice. I mentioned that it had all been my idea, that Amir had nothing to do with it. He then spoke to Amir and handed him a tissue to clean up the blood from his thumb.

The client representative, one of the high-level managers, showed up sometime after ten. He refused to shake my hand or Amir's and went in the security guard's little box office to have a chat with Liam. After twenty minutes they were both out, smiling and moaning about the live football match on TV they had been forced to skip in order to be there.

The representative ensured the security guards that Amir and I had authorization to enter the site at any time. He mentioned that he would send the security company the paperwork the following day.

After a short conversation about the incident with the security guards, he advised the cut open section of the fence be immediately repaired and that work continued as normal. 'Big drama means little work' he said, and they all seemed to agree with him.

After the client representative left the site, Liam asked us to join him for a drink. We agreed without hesitation, even though we were shattered. I followed his car without much zest, as he drove to one of the city's favorite pubs.

We all sat at the bar and began to talk about the incident. Amir and I became chattier after a few pints of beer and looked slightly relieved. Liam liked that. He ordered more drinks for us and listened a lot more than he talked.

After more than two hours at the pub, I finally asked Liam if he could give us a lift back home. I was tired and dizzy from the alcohol and also felt that Amir was still devastated by the incident. He was sipping beer like water.

Liam first dropped Amir at his flat and then, as I was explaining to him the easiest way to get to my apartment from there, he stopped the car, turned off the engine and gave me a long, icy look, the look of disappointment. He took a deep breath, pushed his shoulders back on the seat and looked me straight in the eyes.

'Sharron, do you realize what you have done tonight? You have almost jeopardized our relationship with the client. This could have had tremendous consequences for the project, for all of us. You were lucky the client rep was an old friend of mine and had that much common sense to see this was a child's game.'

'I am sorry. I didn't intend to cause such a stir. I am really sorry.'

'I just can't see why you did that. It is so much unlike you. You are always controlled, cautious. Was this Amir's idea and you just went along with it?'

'No, it wasn't like that. It was my idea.'

'All right, if you say so. Let's get you home. We'll talk again on Monday.'

I nodded my head, relieved I was finally heading home. He turned the engine on and drove down the main avenue of the city. The lights from the street were reflected on the car window like anguished tiny fireflies persisting to survive in the black night.

'Here you go.' He said, as the car pulled up in front of the apartment complex where I lived. 'I will ask you not to talk to anyone about the incident tonight. This is what I agreed with the client rep. It is better this way, there is already too much nonsense going on at work.'

I nodded without looking at him as my shaky hand searched for the car door handle. Liam sighed lightly before placing both hands nervously on the steering wheel; his body language indicating we were not yet done.

'I believed in you, Sharron.' He finally murmured, keeping his eyes fixed on the car windscreen. 'I hoped you could do great things. Remember what I said to you the day we had lunch together at the "Grand Burger"? What we do here is not just about us, it is about others around us too. People we work with are affected by our actions... You understand that? Today, you could have ruined both your career and Amir's. You get how serious that is, don't you?'

He turned his head towards me and I kept mine down, my eyes pinned on my jeans, my right hand clutched on the car door handle.

'I know. I am sorry... I am really sorry.' I finally said, hoping he would stop it there.

'Why do you think I gave Amir to you? So that you could teach him, show him that what we do here has purpose, it is not just some kids' adventure park. It was your chance to make a difference, to help someone grow in the company. You need to understand that you have to be an example to him, not a mindless burrow digger. Is that how you see yourself?' His voice had suddenly got louder.

I let go of the car door handle and turned my head towards the car window, away from him. The lights from the street looked brighter than before.

'I am so sorry... I am not that good at making a difference. I find it difficult to strive.' I mumbled slowly.

'Why not?' He snarled. 'What do you have to lose? Why not give it a try for a change? You want to remain a burrow digger all your life? Crawling on security fences like a rat?'

'I am really, really sorry for that.'

'Stop apologizing. You need to change, you understand? No one is ever going to trust you, if you continue like that. You can do all the hard work in the world, yet no one is going to trust you with real responsibility at work and it is not just that. No one is going to count on you as a friend either.' He shouted, his face almost touching my hair.

'I think... I think you never really trusted me. You made Amir work with me, so he could keep me on track...So that I would not crack in a moment of instability...' I muttered without moving a muscle in my face. 'Deep inside, you expected me to fail. And you used Amir... You used him as my pillar, to help keep me upright.'

I sensed the clear shock in his eyes as I gasped out those words. His hands started to shake. He wasn't expecting it; he was clearly at a loss for words.

'There's nothing wrong with that, a lot of people would have done the same in your place.' I continued, still looking at the lights from the street. 'You have to do what you think is best for the company…But, I worked hard here, I really did, regardless of my personal issues…

And I thought that as a recognition for my hard work, you gave me the opportunity to mentor someone, to hold their hand. But it was the other way around, it seems… Anyways, I better leave now. I better leave. Dubai was a bad idea.' I said and opened the car door.

I entered the apartment complex from the back door, the one I normally used, and pressed the elevator button. The hall was dark and empty, which was usual for that time of the day. I pushed myself against the wall and waited for the elevator to come down. I could still feel the taste of salty gravel in my throat, the mud from the site on my face. I closed my eyes, feeling broken to pieces and longed for a bath. At that moment, Bob's words advising me not to relocate to Dubai flashed in my mind. He had been right all along; for the move to Dubai, for not seeing a psychiatrist and for everything else.

I noticed the main hall lit up as someone walked hastily in the building. I didn't want to be seen in that state by any of my neighbors, so I got in the elevator and quickly pushed the button that led to the seventh floor, where my apartment was.

I opened my eyes as the door finally began to close and, in that instant, in that tiny fraction of the second, I saw him reach for the elevator. Too late though. The door shut on his face, and I remained numb, dazzled by his loving eyes which screamed guilt, as the elevator took off.

Great Falls Town, 24 December 2007

'Can we exchange presents?' Little Bobby asked, once Christie left the house. I could still hear Mr. Jones' car taking a turn on our driveway and mother's loud laughter, as she chatted to grandma at the front door. Bobby was quick; he had grabbed Christie's presents the minute she left the living room and opened them instantly. Now, he was sitting on my bed, panting for breath, his eyes screaming some sort of urgency.

I finished tidying up the stack of pillows on my bed and then turned to him.

'Don't you like Christie's present? What did she get you?' I asked with little enthusiasm.

'She got me a racing car. But I already have one. You can keep it until my old car breaks down, and then you can give it back to me. I will then return you the pencils.'

'Sounds like a good plan. What did she get me?'

'Pencils, I said. She got you pencils, so you can write in your diary, now that your brain isn't well.'

'Who's said my brain isn't well?'

'Grandma did. But you don't need the pencils, because you like to use pens. I am a million percent sure; you always use pens.'

'All right, just give me the card then. You can have them.'

'Okay, but the card says you can use the pencils to write in your diary, but you don't need them because you have so many pens.'

'Okay, you naughty boy, just give me the card. Happy?'

'Yes,' He said and stormed off the room, only to show up a few seconds later with a box of black and yellow striped pencils and a greeting card.

'I will try the car first, and then I will decide if I want to keep it.' He said, looking a little disappointed. Apparently, the pencils had suddenly lost their magic.

'You can have them both.' I said. 'Now give me the card, please.'

He smiled, happy for his little victory. He handed me the card, gave me a quick kiss on the cheek and ran to the living room.

Great Falls Town, 30 December 2007

On December 30, Christie called me and asked if I wanted to join her on New Year's Eve for lunch at the restaurant. This time they were hosting a buffet party for Great Falls Town municipality staff. She said there would be plenty of good food and music for us to indulge ourselves in.

I wasn't very confident my ears could tolerate the loud music, but nevertheless, agreed to it. I thought it would be a good idea to meet her again, to allow things to patch up between us.

There was a slight chance that if she saw me, sitting at Mr. Jones' table by the fireplace, she would abandon those self-inflicted, revengeful thoughts that had clogged up her brain. Things would then go back to how they used to be a few months ago. We would be two happy, young girls, drinking hot chocolate and dreaming of something bigger than our small hometown. But for now, I had to wake her up from the spell that Anthony McAlester had cast on her. He had most definitely won a battle by poisoning her mind, but he was not going to win the war. As long as I remained close to Christie, there was still hope I could bring her to her senses.

Mother did her usual thing when I mentioned I was going to visit Christie. She panicked and started to walk up and down the room, imagining scenarios where I could suddenly have bad migraines and faint or have my fractured arm hurt by some drunken man. She mentioned that the restaurant would be overcrowded, that Christie would be working in the kitchen and Mr. Jones arranging the tables, so no one would be looking after me.

In the end, after the usual twenty-minute argument, she agreed to give me a lift. This time, however, I made it clear that she was not allowed to step inside Paradise Restaurant, nor was she allowed to tell anyone to look after me. She had to behave normally, just like I had instructed her.

Great Falls Town, 31 December 2007

It hadn't snowed for a few days, so the roads in the town were largely open. Mother was happy about that; she hated driving on icy roads. That disappointed me slightly, because I had always wanted to see snow for New Year's Eve. None of the fireworks or good parties ever impressed me, but I would give everything I had to watch the harmonic flakes of snow fall to the ground as the clock hands lazily crawled to the next year.

That morning, the radio said that for the first time in twenty years, Great Falls Town would not see any snow for New Year's Eve. That's one of the things we are all to be blamed for; I said to myself, sad by the sudden shift in weather.

As we drove down the high street, a few youngsters at the side of the road waved at us. They were building what looked to be a rounded snowman. I waved back and looked at them, hoping I could recognize someone from school. None of them looked familiar. 'Another thing that's not the same anymore', I moaned to myself. 'The world moves on, even when you are stuck in a small room for days. No one waits for you to get better, things just carry on.'

We arrived at the restaurant some time before noon. I wasn't sure why, but the short drive from my house to the restaurant made me feel upset. It was probably the fact that the town looked different from the last time I had been out of the house, or that the frail patches of snow were dying on the pavements that gave me the blues. Or maybe, it was just the anxiety of meeting Christie in her own territory.

Despite the melancholy, upon getting off the car and seeing the flickering lights and Christmas decorations covering the restaurant windows and door, my mood turned around. I suddenly experienced that old sentiment of love and warmth, similar to the flavors of buttery cakes combined with the crispy scent of wood burning slowly in Mr. Jones' fireplace.

I paced towards the restaurant like a bullet, discarding mother's efforts to repeat the same instructions I had been listening to for the last twenty minutes.

The twins were at the bar when I entered the restaurant. They hurried towards me once they got a glimpse of me, smiling and lifting their arms in the air as they talked over each other. Nick helped take my coat off, while Tom showed me to Mr. Jones table.

Tom then asked what I was having, and I, as a loyal costumer would, answered, 'The usual drink, Tom. Please.'

You see, I told myself, some things never change. The twins, for example, they haven't changed a bit. And I am sure neither has Christie. It is only in my head; it is all in my head. The accident has confused all of us; I am sure she will soon get back to her true self.

As I waited for the hot chocolate, I noticed at the center of the room – the long, antique style table that Mr. Jones used only on rare occasions – abuzz with municipality staffers.

There were around twenty of them, all enjoying some good wine, in the company of grilled shrimp and fresh fish, that Mr. Jones would have sourced himself. Christie was right; the food on the table looked delicious and what was more, it smelled delicious too.

I looked around, hoping to spot her somewhere, and as I turned my head towards the kitchen door, I spotted a spruce instead, an unusually large one, with long green branches and sharp pointed needles, almost identical to the one I had seen at St. Thomas church.

Oddly enough, the spruce looked like a figure coming out of a literature book; some sort of a gawky knight pinpointing a sharp, ready to strike sword at me. I don't know why I had that ill sentiment; it was just a freshly cut spruce after all. What was it then? I couldn't tell. I looked at it again, this time without prejudice and God, it struck me then. Things had really changed. That spruce had made it into Mr. Jones' restaurant, inside our conversations, laughs, troubles and worries. It was part of our lives now. He was part of our lives now.

I pursed my lips and looked down on the white table cloth, trying to convince myself that with all the pills I was taking, my head wasn't clear enough to be thinking properly.

When I looked up, she was standing in front of me, her eyes monitoring every single muscle in my face. For some strange reason, she was being dead quiet.

'Why are you sad again?' Christie groaned and looked me straight in the eye.

'I am not sad, just thinking.' I said, a little surprised she had caught me off guard.

'Okay, what are you thinking about then?' She said and turned her head in the direction of the spruce. 'Oh, it's that thing, isn't it? Just let it go for now... Will you, please?'

She paused for a second and then quickly changed her mind. She wasn't going to wait for my response, it was more a rhetorical question. 'Anyways, how are you? Feeling better?' She asked as she turned around, her voice becoming a little softer.

'Yeah, I am feeling better. But, that thing...' I said and pointed towards the spruce at the end of the room. 'It is almost identical to the spruce I saw at the church of St. Thomas. Is it from him?'

'Oh, please, stop it. You know the answer, Sharrie. I am not in the mood for that today. It's New Year's Eve, for God's sake.'

I remained silent. I suddenly felt my wings clipped, the fresh smell from the shrimps around me gone. Christie noticed my pale face and quickly tried to redeem herself. 'Listen, can we forget about him, at least for one day? We can talk about it next month. You know, you are giving him too much credit, girl. He is not that important.' She said and looked around us, a little worried someone might have heard what she had just said. 'Oh, by the way, I loved your Christmas present, very pretty shoes. I am going to wear them at school. Did you like my pencils? Sorry, I have had so many expenses lately and was a bit tight on cash.'

'I actually quite like them,' I said truthfully. 'However, I hope I won't have to write in that diary for too long.'

'Oh honey, I didn't mean it like that. I meant it this way: With pencils, you can write stuff, and, if you later, for whatever reason, regret what you've put down, you can erase it. You know, what is it that Father George says? The truth is not one person's exclusivity, right? With time, you can see things differently. You don't need to have all that negative stuff in black and white forever.'

'You are right, I suppose. I might start using them. Anyways, it's not negative stuff that I am writing, it's the truth. But as I promised you, I won't talk about it today. Well, I have one problem with the pencils, though. Bobby likes them too. He wants to exchange gifts apparently.'

She burst into laughs then. Clearly, she wasn't expecting that.

Christie was very attached to little Bob. She had lost her mother at a very young age, and little Bob was very similar to her in that respect. I always thought that she related to Bob and even felt sorry for him somehow.

'Oh, that little man, I adore him. He is such a prince.' She chuckled. 'One day, he'll become just like my dad, you'll see. Extortive and preacher at the same time.' She smirked and put her soft hand on the table.

'I hope not. At least he doesn't like going to church.' I grinned; a bit amazed by Christie's rich vocabulary.

Christie giggled louder this time. The municipality staffers turned around to look at her for a second and then returned to their own, quiet gossip.

'Oh yeah, he'll find another religion to run you ladies worse than my dad's.' She said and continued to giggle. 'But I doubt he'll ever beat the great Vince Jones. No one comes close to him. He's unique. He's got it all, not just the religion tic but the grumpiness and seriousness and the social awkwardness that comes with it.'

I didn't say anything back because I knew that she wasn't being fair to Mr. Jones. She put her hand over mine, as if to convince me to join her giggles.

146

'Now, Sharrie, look at the woman in the red dress. Do you know her?' She whispered, the corners of her eyes still wrinkled by the laughs and leaned her head to the left, towards the antique style table.

'No, first time I've seen her. Does she work in the municipality?' I asked, without much interest.

'Well, she is the mayor's wife. And the guy on her right is her lover. He works with her husband, you see. And he is younger than her, by the way.' She lowered her voice and bit her lower lip hard.

'Oh lord. Good gossip you have here for New Year's Eve table.' I sniffed, a little ironically. She frowned and pushed her hair behind her shoulders.

'Do you know where father is? What do you think? Where is he?' She asked theatrically.

I shrugged, glancing around the room one more time.

'I tell you.' She smirked. 'He is hiding in the kitchen, because he doesn't want to say hello to the mayor's wife. He thinks he will go to hell if he becomes part of such injustice.'

'I see. That's a bit overstretched though, isn't it?

'Oh honey, you know father. He is so conservative when it comes to such matters. I told him - it's none of our business. You need to get out and say hello to the mayor and his wife, for the sake of the business. They are good customers. We have three to four events like this in the year. He said no, he's not going to greet them. Doesn't want to be part of the theatre, he said. So now, he has locked himself in the kitchen... Tell me, how can I fix this man? How can I bring him to the fucking twenty-first century?'

'Oh dear, I will go inside to say hello then.'

'Go ahead, then. You are always nice to him, anyways. Don't know why, though. I am always rude to your dad; I don't even greet him when he comes here.

'Oh, come on now, how can you say that? I am always on your side. What do you want me to do? I will try to change his mind, okay? I will just go to the kitchen now.'

'Okay, then. Give it a go. Just, careful with your arm, the kitchen door is very narrow…And come quick, the hot chocolate will get cold by then.' She said and changed her voice to sound softer.

I nodded and headed to the kitchen. On the way, the mayor's wife, a chubby woman in her mid-40s, looked at me pitifully. She had heard of the accident, and felt, like most others, that I was alive by some kind of miracle. She looked like a good, kind person.

I found Mr. Jones in the kitchen, cutting potatoes with his left hand. I laughed at first; the sight of him trying to grip the potato with his broken right hand, whilst cutting it with the left, was hilarious. He smiled when he saw me laugh, clearly exhausted by the unsuccessful endeavor.

'How are you, my dear?' He said joyfully, looking rather tired.

'I am better, thanks. Shall I help you with that?' I said and pointed at the potato bag.

'Oh, two half hands can't make up for one.' He joked, and moved to the kitchen sink to wash his hands.

'Mine is almost recovered.' I said confidently.

He looked back at my arm. The sunlight from the kitchen window which sank peacefully on his face, had suddenly made his wrinkles look deeper and wider, like canyons of a dead river.

'Are you still having migraines?' He asked bluntly. 'Does the music here disturb you? I can tell the boys to turn it off.'

'No, I am good. The music doesn't really bother me much, nor does the sunlight.' I lied and he nodded his head as if he believed me.

We were still talking about my recovery, when Mrs. Elliott followed by Christie walked into the small hall of the kitchen. They looked nervous; clearly, they had been discussing something before opening the door and had suddenly stopped.

'The mayor's wife has asked to see you.' Christie announced loudly and dumped the tray of plates on the table.

'Please Mr. Jones, I believe it is better you see her.' Mrs. Elliott intervened softly and placed her old, big hand on her pink cheek.

'Yes', I added. 'It is New Year's Eve; it is nice to greet the customers.'

'What does she want now?' Mr. Jones grumbled, rattled by the insistence.

'Mr. Jones, she just wants to say thank you, I believe, right, Christie?' Mrs. Elliott replied steadily, as if weighing up each word that came out of her mouth.

'Tell her to thank God for the food on her table, and for everything else she has got. Not me.' He snapped.

Mrs. Elliott looked stunned. The ceiling had suddenly fallen on her and she couldn't move. She brought her hand from the cheek down to her mouth, fully covering it with her old, swollen fingers, as her lips muttered feebly a silent prayer from beneath. Christie was mad with rage.

'Dad, what's wrong with you? It is New Year's Eve.' She yelled. 'Can't you pretend to be normal for once? For God's sake, you are such an embarrassment.'

'Young girl, don't you dare disrespect me like this.' He yelled back, pointing his shaky index finger at her. 'This is my house, my rules. You do what I say, not what you please. Do you understand that?'

He stiffly chucked the potato into the bin, took a deep sigh and continued, this time in a lower tone. 'You can give whatever excuse you want to that whore, I am going out for a cigarette. When I return, I want none of this circus being talked of again.' And without saying another word he stormed off from the room.

I did finally have the hot chocolate, which had turned cold by the time I returned to the table. Christie sat opposite me, dismissive of the twin's looks begging her to help with customers. Before we sat down, we had been to see the mayor's wife. I had witnessed Christie's discomfort while she had been cooking up stories, trying to justify her father's absence. She was now resting defeated in the chair in front of me, her Christmas jumper glittering happily, as the last happy token of a bad day.

'You know what?' She mumbled, after a short pause. 'I think I am going to come to your place for dinner tonight.'

She then took a sip of her hot chocolate, after which a dark mark was left on the corners of her mouth. She didn't clean it up, reminding me that she was still a little girl, lost between the world of the grownups and ours.

'Better you stay with your father this time.' I said confidently and sipped some hot chocolate myself. 'He spent Christmas alone; it is not fair he also spends New Year's Eve by himself.'

'He's brought that to himself.' She frowned. 'Look at his behavior, Sharrie. He is acting like a child. What can I do to bring him to his senses? I am fed up with him. Totally fed up.'

'I know you are. He is so old fashioned when it comes to such silly things. It is none of his business what other people do, anyways. He's acting as if he is on some mission to purify the world.'

'Exactly! Outworn, provincial nutter, that's what he is. He thinks the world revolves around this little town, around this little restaurant. Doesn't know how the real world works. Who on earth does he think he is to decide what is wrong or right? Everyone should live their lives the way they choose. I say to hell with him. To hell with him, Sharrie.'

'Calm down, now. Have some hot chocolate.' I said and poured some water in her glass. 'Okay, you can come to my house tonight. You can sleep over. Knowing you, I think, he won't mind.'

She nodded her head and smiled, a little relieved.

I noticed the restaurant was getting busier at that point, but she still didn't mind it; she continued to sip calmly her hot chocolate.

'I will just go to the restroom first.' I said, feeling the noise around us getting louder.

'Sure thing.' She smiled and flickered her fingers on the table. She was nervous, no doubt, and probably still angry too.

I gave Christie a light pat on the shoulder as I moved off my seat. She didn't move, just pursed her lips and continued to sip her hot chocolate.

I passed through the main hall of the restaurant, where municipality staffers were now loudly chatting and joking with one another. One of the twins stopped me in the hall and asked if I wanted anything brought to the table. I shook my head and continued to walk towards the end of the room. The tall spruce stood silent ahead of me, this time looking strangely shy. I thought it had been silly of me to compare it to an armed knight pinpointing some ferocious sword at me. In fact, the tree was quite beautiful and actually smelling of heaven, like all spruces did. I would have surely loved it, I thought, hadn't it been from that pervert.

I pushed the door that led to the tiny corridor, at the end of which two piney doors stood silent in the dark. I accelerated my pace towards the women's restroom and once I pushed it, it hit me; that evil sword came sneakily from behind me and hit me. It hit me so effortlessly and brutally that I had no time to react. It hit me on the back, like all traitors do.

Dubai, December 2018

'He's saved me, he's brought me back.' I thought to myself, as I stood still in a corner of the room, watching him slowly button up his clean, white shirt. Against all odds and despite my conviction that the damage that had been done to me could not be undone, he had managed to bring me back. Not from the dead or the crackpots, no, no one could do that; he had brought me back from that long, lonely journey to the past that had tormented me for years. And, oddly enough, it hadn't been that difficult. He had somehow managed to persuade me to jump off the old, smelly train carriage I had been stuck in for years, into a new, clean one, smelling of his fresh cologne.

Shameful as it sounded, Liam had succeeded where everyone else, including mother and Bobby, had failed. It wasn't that he had tried harder than them; on the contrary, I was convinced that Liam had saved me without actually seeking to save me. For the last five months that we had been seeing each other, he had treated me like a slightly introvert, withdrawn girl, who was otherwise perfectly normal.

That was perhaps the reason he had managed to lift me up like no therapist had ever been able to, regardless of their expertise or goodwill. I was convinced that the key to his success had been exactly that: not knowing my history and thus introducing me to a fresh, normal life.

In the past, everyone had been worried that my cracks would propagate to the point I would break into tiny pieces. They had failed to see that sometimes it was better to grab the cracked pot and fill it with water

Hometown Fences

rather than letting it rot in a locked-up cupboard, in a bid to prolong its life.

Liam noticed the absent look on my face and smiled at the mirror in front of him. His smile travelled back to me and dazzled the odd thoughts I was having.

'We are going out tonight. What do you think?' He prompted, staring at me through the mirror. I knew that type of deep look. It meant: Say yes, say yes, please. It is Friday; let's get a drink or two at my favorite pub.

I nodded and smiled back at him. He clearly liked that. He clapped his baby white hands like a happy child, stood up and swiftly disappeared from the room.

I didn't stir. Friday nights out were not my thing and Liam knew that. It wasn't that I didn't like the music or the crowds. On the contrary, I enjoyed all that. What I dreaded, were my previous recollections of nights out.

During my years as a student, I found myself partying and drinking to my limits. That was my release valve, my moment of numbness. That, of course, was true until I would return home from the party. Then, I would lock myself in the bathroom and sob in front of the mirror, quietly eating the lipstick from my lips. I would pinch and bite my arms and cheeks until I would notice giveaway marks. When the pain would become unbearable, I would walk to the balcony overlooking the dorm rooms filled with noisy students.

I would sob there in the dark, looking at the cold, grey pavement below my feet, knowing it was about the right time I ended it there. But I always put it off, thinking I wouldn't like to die looking like a drunken junkie.

The rest of the week would follow with the usual self-loathing and guilt. I would hate myself for having dressed up, put on my red stilettos and laughed over alcohol with people I knew very little about. I would dread the conversations, the giggling, the touching, the sweaty breaths and kisses and the euphoria alcohol had brought about. I would promise to myself that I would never do it again. And yet, I would do the same the following week.

Now I was different. I was grown up. The drinking had stopped and the self-loathing had faded out. The Friday nights out were nothing like those in the past; in fact, I felt, they were a test of confidence. A test, which I was always unwilling to take, but always managed to pass when I did.

Liam was now back in the room. He was holding a tray, where he had placed a good smelling cheese and ham toast and a glass of orange juice. I felt blessed to have him.

'Are you okay, hon?' He whispered as he lay the tray on the bed.

I nodded and pushed myself up, smiling at the huge portions of the toast, smelling the cheddar cheese as it sailed through my nose.

'I knew this would cheer you up.' He said and pointed at the fresh toast. 'Better than jam, isn't it?'

'Yup, I love it, I love you.' I smiled and leant forward to kiss him. He smiled back and returned the kiss softly.

'Now, I will see you in the office at the usual time. I hope this early morning meeting will not last too long.'

'All right,' I hummed. 'Did you have something to eat yourself?'

'It's okay, I'll manage with some coffee.' He said and gave me another kiss on the forehead. 'I better get going; I don't want to be late. I will see you in office.'

I parked the car in the building parking lot and started to walk towards the office building. Unlike the first days of the week, Friday had begun like a typical, chilly December day. The pavements still smelled of fresh, night rain and the fragile sun was mostly hidden behind stubbornly rigid clouds.

I had been so used to the sun the last couple of months, that I suddenly felt sad. Watching the sun, like falling in love, had been acts of defiance on my side. Now that I was no longer shying away from it, the sun had decided to take a break from me.

Perhaps it was testing me, hoping I wouldn't bury my head in the sand like in my dark days, where glazing at its rays meant solely pain. Enough with that, I told myself, tired of hyper analyzing the weather. That's one of the things no one can control, and besides, it is December. It can't always be sunny.

I smiled good morning at the building security guard as I walked in the office building and took the elevator up to the second floor. The office was almost empty; it was still very early to be in the office.

I took a seat on my chair and turned on the laptop, before hearing a well-known voice behind my back.

'Good morning, star girl.' Max Tinwell gawked at me half asleep. The smell from his mouth flew through my nose and I suddenly felt sick.

Max Tinwell was the Company's Health and Safety manager for the "New Millennium" project. He usually did not do much, but his presence was always required in meetings, hence he had to travel almost weekly from London to meet up with the clients in Dubai. Busy and loud, he was constantly on the phone, few times talking to colleagues, most times to any of his four children.

There were times when I thought his happy and vital nature was a direct result of his children's influence. I couldn't explain it otherwise, the bizarre hype and excitement, the laughs, the relaxed attitude at work. On a professional note, well...his office was a mess and his reports were always issued late. But no one minded any of that. He was a good person; everyone wanted to hang out with him.

Max had been friends with Liam since they had started out their careers. Liam confided in him; they often went out for long dinners in Dubai's restaurants, or played golf on weekends. Max was also one of the few people in the office who knew about our relationship. I believed he knew a lot about Liam, about his life before me, that is.

'Good Morning Max, good to see you here.' I said, slightly surprised to have seen him in the office that early in the morning. 'How have you been?' I asked, and gently pushed the chair on the side to allow myself some distance from him. Luckily, he didn't notice the move. He came closer, sat on the chair next to mine, put his feet on the desk and mumbled something to me, with a yawn.

I suddenly felt bad for having pushed the chair like that. Poor thing, he looked exhausted. The bags under his eyes were worse than usual, swollen and black. The little hair on the forehead had become whiter from the previous time I had met him.

'When did you arrive?' I said with a soft voice, praying silently that he hadn't come to realize the reason I had pushed the chair away from him so abruptly.

'Some urgent nonsense meeting. I flew in last night... Back to London on Saturday.' He frowned.

'Oh, that's awful. Shall we get some coffee?' I smiled, hoping to change his mood a little.

'Yes, please. I am too early here, anyways. Didn't know they would be caught up in a meeting this early.'

'Yes, another urgent Friday meeting nonsense,' I frowned back and walked behind him.

On the way to the kitchen, we walked past the conference room which was loud with people talking over each other. I could hear Liam's voice coming from the inside, loud and antagonizing. He sounded stern, as ever. Work never got any better, I thought.

Max closed the kitchen door behind him and gave away a phony smile. His cunning, teenage looking eyes almost spoke loudly.

'What's that, star girl? Where is the smile gone? Oh, I know what you are thinking... Let me tell you something then... Don't be upset to hear Liam talk like that. It doesn't bother him. It really doesn't. I mean, on a personal level, what he does here doesn't affect him. He's been doing this job for a long time and he knows how things work. Besides, you have to consider that he is only standing up for his team. The client would have crushed us, if it wasn't for his adamant resistance. We need more people like him; people who can put up a fight against them. The majority of people here is used to simply bending down. And when that happens too often, you can't get any work done.'

I nodded at Max, knowing his words were genuine.

'I don't want him to have a heart attack.' I smiled. 'The pressure is too much; he is constantly stressed.'

Max burst into laughs and came closer to me. 'Sharrooooon! You are already talking like a good, old wifey. Please don't talk to him like that. He'll feel old. I mean, he is quite old compared to you, hah, but he'll feel like a grandpa. Please don't do that to him.'

I smiled back at him. Naughty Max, he could always get away with anything, I thought. 'I don't lecture him on how to do his job,' I persisted. 'It is just that this level of stress can harm him.'

'Now, the only heart attack Liam Monroe can ever have is from you, young lady. I know that for a fact.' He paused, took a sip of his coffee and then continued slowly. 'You know Sharron, when Liam was engaged, he gave it all to his Mrs. Not just his heart, his self-esteem too... And he suffered a lot as a result. He tried everything to make her happy; everything.

I frowned and he felt the need to explain more.

'You see, she wanted to change cities constantly. She was restless, couldn't settle down in one place. And he never said no, he just followed her everywhere. His career became second to hers. She would get a job offer in Geneva and the next day would fly out to move there. Liam had to follow her, if he wanted to make the relationship work. And he did that for almost five years. He moved from one country to another, from one job to another. For her sake. He was truly invested in that relationship.' He said and shook his head with disappointment.

'Now, I think he is doing the same here with you.' Max continued, keeping his eyes locked on the floor. 'You like to take things slowly, which I believe, is something he really appreciates... And, I will say this to you as his friend: Please Sharron, don't break his heart. He doesn't deserve it a second time.'

I nodded and took a sip of the morning coffee which suddenly felt painfully bitter. The confession I had heard a moment earlier had left me a little shocked, but all the same, I decided it was better to say nothing.

I was, however, surprised to learn how well Max knew Liam. They were of similar age and had known each other from a previous job. Liam had mentioned that they used to spend time together, like playing football on weekends on the sunny days of late spring when they were back in London. However, I hadn't realized he knew of Liam's romantic history that well. I was aware that Liam's previous relationship was a bit of a conversation taboo. A few times that I had tried to mention it, he had changed the topic and looked at me with disappointment. So, I had stopped. There was no point to ask any questions about his past, as long as he didn't ask any about mine. It was fair play that way. We both had hidden skeletons in our cupboards, and were not yet ready to reveal them.

'What happened?' I said eventually, when the bitterness of the coffee had flattened out. I couldn't resist asking, I wanted to know more. 'What actually happened between them? He's never said why the whole thing fell apart.'

'That's not my story to tell,' Max smiled a bit anguished. 'But I can ensure you, it wasn't his fault… None of it was. He put too much trust, too much love. In a way, he played with fire and got burned. And, the wounds after that were unbearable.'

'It seems to me as if you are talking about a different person. The Liam I know is full of confidence and life. I cannot imagine him broken from love.' I confessed.

'True. But every wolf has his wounds…. no matter how fearsome or wild. In the beginning, the pain transformed him; he became a mess, a different man. But then, with time, he picked himself together and focused on what he was good at, his work. And, gradually, he built up his confidence, his self-esteem. However, he was not quite the same person he used to be before the engagement.

'He became stiff, almost frosty… He wouldn't smile or crack jokes, he wouldn't even join us for our Sunday football matches. That, of course, all changed when he met you…' He paused a little and then took a slow step closer. 'He is healing now. You have brought him back, Sharron. So, keep up the good work.' The yellow teeth showed up from behind his lips as his smile took over his face. Max then raised his coffee mug as if raising a toast and took a long, coke like sip.

I stood there puzzled. I wanted to ask Max more questions, things like: Had they been in love? What had she done to make him suffer like that? Was she now settled with a different man? These questions had been troubling me for some time, and I was now more eager than ever to know the truth. But I also knew that none of the things I was hoping to learn would make me feel better. So, I thought, it was wiser to just not ask any more questions.

Listening to Max talk like that, I felt proud of Liam. He had learnt to let go. Unlike me, he had kept his skeletons locked away in his attic cupboards, decorated with leaves of lavender and dressed in colorful clothes, so they wouldn't intimidate him. One day, when he would be ready, he would burn them, or, if still sentimental about them, bury them with some decency. It was not the case for me.

I had been hoping the skeletons would decide to leave my cupboards quietly one night and never return. But they were so used to my company that they decided to spend the rest of their time with me. The truth was, like most of us, they also longed for someone to remember them. And the only way they knew to do that was to drag their victims into horror. Not because they wanted to harm them in any way, but only because they wanted someone to hang out with.

'Do people in the office know you two are hanging out?' Max interrupted the odd silence.

'Hmm, here and there they know. Amir knows, and maybe a couple of his friends. But we wouldn't like to rush things; so, we haven't been loud about it.'

'Totally get it. Good stuff.'

'Yup. Listen, are you free tonight? We are going to the King Arthur Castle pub in downtown this evening, around nine thirty.'

He smiled. 'King Arthur Castle pub in Dubai? You bet I am. They better serve some decent ale there.' He said and sipped some more of his coffee.

I had asked Amir to join us after work at the King Arthur Castle pub, which was right in the center of town, and usually flooded with tourists and expats.

Liam was slightly late to pick me up. He looked tired, which was a sign of a long and nasty day at work. He had bought some salad and crisps at the supermarket and asked if I wanted to have some food in the car, before going to the pub. After the pub, we had planned to go to his apartment. We would order Sushi and watch a movie.

Even though we had been seeing each other for a few months, Liam and I hadn't moved in together. We still liked to spend weekends, and occasionally weekdays, at each other's places though. Usually, it was me going to his place. There were fewer ghosts there, and of course more space for both of us.

After the third month, he insisted I moved in with him, but I had asked for more time. He had not pushed me further, hoping I would change my mind after Christmas.

Now that December was here and the sun had started to hide behind dense clouds, I had decided to say yes. I would tell him after the pub tonight, when we would be alone at his place. I was ready, after hearing what Max had to say, I was ready. I was ready to let go and start over. With the man I loved.

'You look pretty tonight,' Liam smiled shyly as he kissed me. 'You never wear red lipstick. It suits you.'

'Thanks, I thought I would try it out.' I said, feeling a bit uneasy.

'Good, well done. And high heels too, that's a good surprise. Is that all for me?'

'Yeah, it's for both of us.' I said and leant over to kiss him on the cheek.

Liam grew happier. He pressed the gas pedal, turned the music up and began to sing alongside the vocalist on the radio. I looked outside the window, as the lights from the highway twinkled in the distance, shyly piercing the darkness of the night and smiled to myself. He could be quite theatrical when he wanted, I thought, and kept my head against the window, worried my smile would discourage him.

At some point, I realized that I hadn't had anything to eat since breakfast, so I turned around to the back seat and seized the supermarket bag that Liam had brought with him. I grasped a pack of biscuits and started to chew in silence, enjoying Liam's singing tune as Dubai's high-rise buildings passed by like frozen princesses.

Life can be ironic at times. Over and over again it traps you into similar situations; situations that make you believe that this time around you have a choice, you can make a difference. And then it slaps you in the face, to tell you that despite your choices and actions, you are very little to change things. Because life always decides for you, not once, not twice but as many times as it bloody wishes.

We never made to the pub that night. Bob's text was short. 'Grandma is gone. Fly out tonight, if you can.' It was then that I realized the taste of almonds in my mouth, Liam's croaky singing, the frozen look of the buildings around me. I spat the biscuits on my lap and asked Liam to turn around.

We made it to the airport around 11:00 p.m. The last two hours had passed very quickly; I could barely remember what I had packed in my bag. Time around me had stopped; I was mentally back in my small hometown, the itchy taste of almonds in my throat wrecking my nerves with pleasure.

Liam had been bizarrely quiet. He hadn't said much on the way to the airport and now that we were standing in the departures area, he was constantly checking gate numbers on the screen above him. He felt uncomfortable with my numbness and didn't know what to do.

'Would you like me to come with you?' He finally said with some hesitation. 'I can stay in a hotel in town, until you are done. And then perhaps we can go on a short trip together...'

He said the last words with little hope; I could tell by the forced smile on his contorted face.

'Not this time.' I said lethargically. 'I have to be alone this time.'

'I understand.' He continued; the forced smile on his face now vanished. 'We can do the trip when you come back, what do you think?'

I nodded insincerely.

'All right, then,' He said and took a step closer to me. 'You take care of yourself, will you?'

He then squeezed me into his arms; before whispering to my ear. 'And come back to me, okay?'

I gave him a blank look and said nothing.

'Sharrie, I will be here, everyone at work will be here, waiting for you. We need you; I need you.' He whispered into my ear; his hands still clamped on my arms.

I pulled myself from him slowly and gave out a weak nod.

'You don't have to go if you don't want to.' He finally said in a begging tone. 'You can stay here, you know that, right?'

'I have to go,' I said looking up at the display screen.

'Okay, sure. You have got this under control. I trust you. Let's not be late.' He said in a confident tone this time, and lifted my hand luggage.

We walked in silence for a few minutes until we reached the ticket scanning machines.

'I love you, babe.' He said hurriedly and gave me a quick kiss, 'I will call you when you have landed. We'll talk every day, okay?'

'Okay.' I said, a little confused.

'Very well.' He said and pushed the hand luggage to the scanning gate.

I walked through the gate and turned my head to wave goodbye at him, only to realize he had my red lipstick on his lips.

That lipstick somehow gave me the chills. I suddenly forgot what I had wanted to tell him.

Great Falls Town, 19 December 2018

The airport of Great Falls Town was all covered in snow, just as I had seen it the last time I was in town, which was over six years ago. The walkways around the airport were also buried in fresh, fluffy snow which had fallen the night before and hadn't yet cleared up.

It was 4:10 a.m. when I landed and all shops and restaurants inside the airport were shut. The information desk, a tiny cabin, which normally was always busy, was also shut. The luggage collection area right in front of the arrivals gates, which in the daytime would buzz with people, was almost empty.

I waited for some ten minutes to receive my luggage and then made my way down the corridor that connected the customs area with the main arrivals hall. It had been covered with a giant wallpaper showing a breathtaking picture of Great Falls Town's highest gorge dropping down the rapid flowing river Charlie.

I pulled with effort the luggage as the wheels rattled with noise on the sloppy pavement, barely imitating the sound of rocks and water being gushed with force down the gorge and into the river.

The arrivals area, all bordered by new transparent windows that oversaw the beautiful Great Falls Town forest seemed smaller than usual; the snow that had covered most of the surroundings limited the view to the forest and made the space inside shrink a little too. As a result, the atmosphere around the hall felt a bit isolating. However, there was that exception I was waiting for that would make all the difference. The six feet tall, kinky snowman at the center of the arrivals hall, all surrounded by glittery Christmas ornaments, that tried hard to stand upright. Only in Great Falls Town you could find a snowman as dressed up as him, as tall as him, as dear as him, I thought.

In the airplane I had a lot of time to think; to sleep of course, as well; but primarily to think. And after thinking hard, sleeping, thinking again, crying and sleeping a bit more, I had woken up to realize that I was actually being a fool. I was in a very good place in my life at the moment. I was blessed to be loved and looked after by people I cared for. And I had to be grateful for that. Period. Now it was time I acted as a responsible person and made up for all the turmoil I had caused.

'Things have changed around here, however not the really good things.' I concluded, as I recognized the soft female voice with a strong Southern accent announce arrival times. 'The good things always stay the same. I love you, dear snowman'. I whispered again, as I headed towards the exit gates.

The cold wind at the exit gate felt like a stony slap on my face, so used by then to the heat of Dubai. It gave me shivers, but for some strange reason it felt good; because it felt like a wake-up type of slap.

With that positive vibe, I made my way to the parking area hoping that I would be able to book a taxi at the local airport taxi service office, which I knew had only a limited number of cabs, and with Christmas at the doorstep, they were probably all taken. Bob had texted to say he wouldn't be able to pick me up, as with mother less mobile, he was in charge of arranging grandma's service. To make things more complicated, for some reason, his Uber account wasn't working either.

I got in the taxi and drove slowly past large service vehicles which were clearing ice from the sidewalks that had packed overnight, just as a happy, loud family with three young children tried to make their way past them into their parked car.

It was always the case during this time of year. Students, soldiers, big city professionals, all came back to Great Falls Town to celebrate Christmas. The town looked different for those few days. The main promenade, right by the lake, was flocked with people strolling up and down, looking for places to spend their time. The traffic in the city got really bad, almost as bad as in the summer.

Restaurants and cafés were crowded. I knew this very well, because at Paradise Restaurant, work doubled during Christmas time. Mr. Jones always ran out of staff, to the point that I had to help in the kitchen whenever I visited.

Now that the taxi was moving slowly through the cracky ice crystals, I realized that we were only a few blocks from Christie's restaurant. My heart dropped on the floor.

We approached the town center and as the recently finished high-rise building shadowing the promenade cleared out of view, there it appeared. That old standing castle of mine, which corners I knew inside out, was shimmering in bright lights. The good things always stay the same, I thought, and took a deep breath.

A tall spruce stood proudly outside the entrance door of the restaurant, all covered in layers of beaming lights. New, big tree, I thought. It would look better if it didn't block all the windows, I moaned to myself.

Slightly disappointed from the restricted view, I turned my head up front, towards the icy road ahead of us.

The taxi drove straight past the promenade, leaving behind the shimmering lights of the restaurant and I, for the first time in years, longed for the taxi to speed up.

'I need to write to Liam. He must be worried by now'. I suddenly realized, as my feet started to feel the freezing cold, penetrating through the thin car parquet.

It was quite embarrassing for me what had happened at the airport. I had been such an idiot. I thought that when I landed in Great Falls Town, he would evaporate from my memory, like everything else before him. In my mind, Great Falls Town was where my real life was happening, where my soul was trapped. And when I was there, everything else turned into dust.

I repeated the last few words a couple of times before realizing that I was actually wrong. Very wrong. Liam would never be busy enough to not remember me. He would not think about me during his hectic days, but I knew that when he had a moment alone, in between meetings or calls, he would think of me and smile.

I felt that for the first time perhaps, I really missed him. I missed him for telling me what to wear in the mornings, what to do in my empty evenings, how to correctly cook the pasta, how to save my money or fix the bathroom door handle. I missed him for all the earthly things I had no interest in, before knowing him.

I searched for my phone in the almost empty backpack and texted him. "I have landed, on my way home. Missed you. Love." And then waited anxiously for his reply.

Great Falls Town, 31 December 2007

I don't know for how long I had been in the dark, until I felt a soft tap on my shoulder. I raised my head to notice the curious and partly worried look of a girl, who was asking in a bleak voice if I was okay. She must have been around ten but looked quite tall for her age.

'I will go get some help. I will be right back.' She whispered with the confidence of a grown up.

'No, please,' I blurted in pain. 'I will get up by myself. I just need to get to the restroom.

'All right', she said convinced, and gave me her hand to pull me up. 'I will wait here until you finish.'

I thanked her shyly and walked into the restroom where I immersed my face into the freezing cold tap water until I felt none of the muscles in my face.

Fifteen minutes later I was standing outside the front door of Paradise Restaurant, anxiously waiting for Christie, who had gone to ask permission from Mr. Jones to spend New Year's Eve with me, while my head continued to spin around in pain.

Mr. Jones had been busy at the back of the restaurant unloading fresh fish from the truck that had just arrived from local fishermen boats. At this time of the year, he needed to load on fresh bass and trout twice a day.

I was glad everyone at the restaurant was busy and didn't notice what happened to me at the restroom.

The little tall girl was still staring at me from her table. She had a worried look; the type of look you get when someone gives you an unconvincing excuse such as bad migraines. She must have assumed I had been drinking alcohol secretly, considering I was hanging out with the restaurant owner's daughter.

The taxi had by then arrived and was parked a few feet away from me. I could now spot Christie coming down the stairs with her purple coat on and a bag, which I thought was full of fresh sweets, baked by Mrs. Elliott.

'All sorted.' She yelled as she slammed the door behind her, clearly in high spirits. 'I told dad I am staying over at your place tonight. I am sure we will have a great night! He will come tomorrow at 8 a.m. to pick me up. Walla!' She pronounced the last word in a different accent, one of her many ways to make something sound more exciting.

'Nice', I added. 'Was he upset though?'

'Upset, for what? He will be with Nick, Tom and Mrs. Elliott over here.' She said. 'Plus, all the customers. It is "business as usual" for him. No day is too special.'

'That's a bit harsh.' I added, my head still spinning around. 'Don't be sarcastic today, it is New Years' Eve.'

'Ok, Sister Sharron, I will keep my mouth shut for the rest of the evening. Now, finally we are free. Shall we get going?'

'Yep, sure.' I said and headed slowly to the back of the taxi.

'You don't look very well, are you okay?' She said and looked me straight in the eye, as the taxi had just started off.

'Yup, it was freezing outside, waiting for you to put your shiny lip-gloss on.' I smirked, pointing at her lips and she liked it.

'It wasn't the lip-gloss that took me so long… It was father. You know how he is; wanted to know what time to come and pick me up tomorrow morning.

'Ahem.' I nodded sarcastically, but she didn't bother to return the irony. 'It is not that chilly though.' She continued. 'Look, there isn't even that much snow on the sidewalks. Are you saying this little cold wind is too much for you?'

'It's supposed to be snowing heavily from tomorrow onwards,' The taxi driver spoke up and Christie and I looked one another in the eye: 'Hello there, someone has been listening all along…'

'Yes, I heard that,' Christie confirmed and turned around to face the road ahead. 'It will be snowing heavily especially up in the mountain.'

'Yes, God knows how long it will take them to clear the roads this time.' The driver complained. 'No one wants to work overtime during Christmas, the young people do not care for the community anymore, just themselves.' He said and turned the heating up.

When we approached the roundabout that led to my house, Christie looked me again in the eye.

'Sharrie,' she said hesitantly, 'I need to deliver some food to one of our customers who is staying at the Marriott Hotel. Do you mind if we drop you first and then come back to your place? It is only a ten-minute drive from your house, I won't be long.'

'Are you serious?' I asked, my eyes zoomed out with clear shock, baffled by her courage to lie to me like that. 'Do you expect me to believe you now?'

'Sharrie, please stop it.' She continued; looking nervously at the driver and then back at myself. 'Honestly, just stop it. I will go back to the restaurant, if you don't.'

'Oh my God, you are such a liar. You had planned this whole thing from the beginning. I can't believe you used me like this.' I yelled.

'Will you please stop?' She yelled back at me. 'I am going back to the restaurant, all right?'

By that time, the taxi had stopped in front of my house. The driver kept both hands on the steering wheel, clearly not knowing what to do next.

'Fine', I said. 'I will get off now. Just don't be late!'

'Good, I won't, an hour or two at most. Erm... you know what to tell father if he calls asking to speak to me, right?' Christie asked, biting her lower lip with anxiety.

'Sure, I know. You are not the only one who knows how to make up stories.' I said and gave her a hateful look.

'Good.' She said with an instant, cunning smile and opened the bag that Mrs. Elliott had given her.

'Fuck this. Just go to hell,' I said abruptly and merged out of the taxi in haste.

'Sharrie, wait,' Christie shouted from the car. 'Won't you take the sweets?'

I didn't turn around to see her. I walked straight into the house, slamming the door behind me with rage.

Great Falls Town, Vermont, 19 December 2018

Grandma's funeral service started slowly. The local Catholic priest, the only one in Great Falls Town, had managed to show up at the cemetery an hour late. Now that he was here, he had clamped himself in a rusted metallic chair, provided last minute by Bob after complaining that he would not be able to deliver the speech standing due to sciatica pain.

Mother didn't look impressed; she wanted her mother to have a decent funeral service and so far, that didn't seem to be the case. She whispered to my ear that the priest was exaggerating the sciatica pain; she had seen him a week earlier run for a charity marathon.

I decided to not fall for her words, primarily because I knew grandma wouldn't have cared less about his speech or anything else related to him or the funeral ceremony for that matter.

The thing was, grandma never had a big thing for religion; as far as I could remember she never went to church – not even during Christmas or Easter, despite being born an Irish Catholic and raised into a reasonably conservative family.

Her ideas of religion contrasted starkly with grandfather's, when it came to the Catholic church. If it wasn't for him; I am sure, we would not be standing in a Catholic cemetery right now and surely, grandma would not have been left waiting to hear a spiritual speech from someone she didn't know.

Grandfather, an army pilot of Polish descent, who fought in the Vietnam war, had met grandma at an army airbase in southern Tennessee, when she had just turned eighteen years old. She was twenty-two years his junior.

Grandma worked at the army base too, but as a clerk; she sent telegraphs up and down the country to notify high grade officers of the progress of war; which regiments would be mobilized next, and so on. Her work was dull, however she often remarked she knew of army secrets few people in the country were aware of.

Despite the stark difference in age, grandma's parents were happy for them to be together, considering granddad's position in society and a good army pension.

Soon after getting married, they had my mother, who would be their only child.

The early years of the marriage were difficult, due to granddad's little talk army style character and the considerable age gap. However, with time, they started to know one another better and seemed to agree on most things; with a rare exception: religion.

Grandfather would often try to talk of his Christian values and why the world would be a better place if all people believed a little bit more. Grandma, brought up in a very American family, who had by then lost touch with their old Irish roots, would have none of that talk.

She was deeply materialistic; she believed you could do good regardless of being a Catholic or not; in fact, she believed that being a Catholic made matters worse as you were inclined to support only the causes that your church supported.

And so, for many years, they argued on that thing; until my grandfather died peacefully on a serene Great Falls Town spring day and grandmother had him buried properly, in a Catholic ceremony. Grandfather passed away slightly disappointed that my mother took after grandma, when it came to spiritual matters, and almost never walked in a church. So, when I was six years old and started attending the local church with Christie, he couldn't be happier. It was half a battle won he said, even though he was still unpleased we couldn't find a local catholic church near our house to go to.

After his death, grandma moved away from Vermont; she relocated down south, to Florida. Her last wish was to be buried alongside her husband; hence we were now all standing in front of a deeply bored Catholic priest.

There were few other people at the cemetery; most of them relatives of an old age and the rest, neighbors or family friends. Father George was amongst them, and I was deeply grateful for his presence there. I knew that my father would not attend the funeral; he had given mother an excuse – traveling for a conference or something. I never expected him to be there and I was sure, neither would grandma, so there were no hard feelings there.

Finally, after a good fifteen minutes of hypnosis, the priest stood up for a second or two, thanked everyone for being there, then sat back down onto his cold chair and started to read from his notes.

Most of the people looked distracted; some of them were clearly not paying any attention to the priest's monologue; some were pounding back and forth in their position, as if begging for it all to end, a few younger relatives who had flown from Florida, were rather amazed by the amount of snow on the wide sidewalks and kept on making remarks to each other about it. It is the drizzling cold - I tried to justify them - it is too cold for them to show dignity and listen in silence.

But then, I looked at the priest's face, cramped with a "get me out of here" expression that I realized the truth.

'It must be Christmas', - I thought - 'that must be it. People don't like the sound of death around Christmas. They wish to completely switch off and celebrate in peace those few days with their loved ones. Dying during Christmas is potentially a sin in itself; in the sense that it deprives people from total, undisturbed happiness.'

'Mad people', I moaned to myself, disappointed that no one was really taking the ceremony seriously, not even the priest himself. 'Soon this will be over, and I will be going home with mother and Bob and a good memory of a good human being who has done nothing wrong, but died during the Christmas season.'

I stared up at the sky; don't know for how long, in a bid to hear the priest's words in silence and when I looked back down at the crowd, I noticed him, a shadow hiding amongst the living; Anthony McAlester. That old, nasty devil was standing somewhere at the end of the crowd of clowns, head down, grey beard touching his chest.

'Oh God', I thought, 'What is he doing here? Why doesn't he just vanish from the surface of earth?'

'Sharrie', Bobby whispered.' The service is about to end now. 'Will you stand by mother and greet everyone? I will need to sort out some work with the priest in the meantime.'

'Yup, sure, go ahead.' I said and took a step closer to mother, who was clearly touched by the priest's words.

Most of the people were done with their chit chats by then; they were all in a hurry to get back to their warm, Christmassy homes, and the ones who weren't, had some flights to catch.

As the crowd withered away, Anthony McAlester approached us, his eyes still jogging around his shoes and the snow around them.

'I am very sorry to hear what happened', he muttered under his breath. 'I hope she will find peace amongst her loved ones.' The last words, he pronounced with a dignified confidence and shook mother's hand.

'I do hope so.' Mother said, touched by his notably honest words.

'Sharron, it is good to have you back in town.' He gasped and gave me his hand but I looked at mother instead. 'Are you planning to stay long?'

His hands were now both buried inside his jacket pockets and he looked so innocent, I almost forgot who I was dealing with. His ravaged face recontoured briefly to release a painful smile.

'No, just a few days only,' I said, still looking at mother.

'Right', he said hesitantly, 'I actually wanted to talk to you. I know it feels very inappropriate now, but if you could spare me five minutes, I would be grateful.'

'I don't believe I have anything to share with you.' I said defensively.

'Sharrie, please', mother pinched me on my arm, 'please for God's sake talk to him. Do it for me.'

'All right, let's go for a walk, but nothing good will come out of this.' I blurted, and looked at mother with hate.

We walked side by side, out of the cemetery and onto the wide sidewalks covered in the thick and sticky December snow.

'Sharron, I have something to show you.' Anthony said after a few minutes of walk without making a sound. His voice was now relaxed, his face contours looked softer. He had aged a lot and didn't look like a happy man any more.

'He took the wallet out of his pocket and showed me the picture of a toddler with big blue eyes and scruffy blonde hair smiling at the camera. 'My daughter; she will be four this summer... Her name is Christiane.' He paused and put his hand over his eyes. 'She is the reason I get by...' He paused again and closed his eyes. 'I just want you to know that there isn't day or night that I don't blame myself for what happened. I hate myself every single minute of the day. So, please blame me and hate me all the way. Because I deserve it. But stop hurting yourself.'

'Why are you showing me a picture of your daughter?' I stopped him; a bit numb from that display of emotion. 'What do you want from me? Sympathy?'

'What I am saying is: Please move on, like the rest of us have... No one is blaming you for what happened; no one. You need to know that. It was a big mistake at a bad time; it had nothing to do with you.

'Okay, thanks for the advice, could you now just piss off and live your happily ever after life as if nothing ever happened?'

'No, I won't, I won't just piss off. Not until we have bottomed this out. You are not the only one who suffered, you know. Just tell me what you wanted to say all along. Just let it out. Why are you so angry with me?'

'Oh, well, for starters, you manipulated a teenager into loving and trusting you. You slept with her and messed with her head. You stole from her. And then, you killed her.'

'Fine; now listen to me. Yes, I did sleep with her. Yes, she helped me out with money which I was going to pay her back later on. But I never manipulated her, you should know that. I opened her eyes; there was more to her life than working as a slave at that shitty restaurant. You can't blame me for telling her she was being exploited when she was supposed to be living her life just like you used to. She was happy with me, Sharron, believe me.

'Oh God, you killed an innocent child, you twisted devil. Keep telling yourself these stories, if you want to feel better at night. Now listen to me for the very last time.' I closed my eyes and took a deep breath, because I knew what I was about to say was beyond myself.

'Do you think I will feel sympathy for you because you have named your daughter Christiane? Or because you are showing me a picture of her ugly looks? How can I, after knowing what you did right after she was gone? You couldn't waste any time, could you? Within eight months, you had to marry the second best looking teenage blondie in town.'

'I married her because she got pregnant.' He frowned, clearly upset. 'And you have no right to call my daughter names; she has nothing to do with any of this. All you…'

'All your family is stained with blood, you murderer!' I interrupted him and walked away with haste.

'Sharron, I don't understand. If it was all my fault and you blame me for everything, why do you keep trying to kill yourself then?' He shouted from behind, his voice now changed to how I remembered it, the vile voice of a sneaky devil. 'Why all the guilt, Sharrie? Why all the bloody guilt?' He came from behind, rushing to catch up with me.

'You must be hiding something, isn't it? What is it that you are hiding, you fucking weirdo? What did you do?' He gasped those words with loud rage, words his heart had been wanting to scream for years, I thought.

His hand was now clinging my arm with force; I tried to pull back but I couldn't. He then grasped both his hands onto my arms and shouted at my face: 'You were the only one who knew where we were that night. Tell me the truth now, what did you do?'

My eyes got blurry, I wished I could become thin air in that moment. I opened my mouth to scream, but my voice was drained, like in some anguishing dream. I stayed there numb, not feeling any pain, just hoping to die, to have never even existed.

He noticed my state of shock and released the compression off my hands. At which point I saw Bob run after him like a mad beast. He pushed through with his full body weight and knocked Anthony down. Anthony resisted, he pulled himself up and managed to catch both Bobby's hands and knocked him down instantaneously, using some sort of professional army tactic. He then ran off to the other side of the road.

Bob went after him, screaming in the distance with all the voice he had.

'I will kill you. If you ever come close to her again, I will kill you.' Bobby shouted. 'I will rip you off, you hear me?'

Anthony did not turn around, he kept running until he disappeared inside the parking lot.

The night that followed was hard work for me. It wasn't the old room, full of skeletons hiding in the corners that gave me shivers; it was Anthony's old looking face, yelling at me. It was the truthful words that came off his heart: 'What are you hiding, what are you hiding?'

Why was it that I felt so guilty? Why hadn't I moved on like everyone else? Was it because I was actually hiding something, something that no one knew, something that tainted me with guilt and thoughts of self-destruction?

I closed my eyes and reassured myself that it was all nonsense; I had now finally matured and grown up; I had met someone who loved me and taught me that we ought to leave the past behind so that others around us can manage to live with us happily. I am staying happy, I thought, not just for me, but for my future self, for my mom, for Bobby and for my love.

As the night cleared from the sky and the first rays of light hit the window of my bedroom, I finally understood that I felt no more hate for Anthony. I felt sorry for him. He had withered into a wretched old man. Deep down inside, I knew that he had suffered a lot. And I was sure he hated himself, but he kept going, he kept living for his family, for his beautiful looking daughter.

'Sharron, please don't leave just yet. Wait until after Christmas.' Mother said, looking desperately heartbroken. 'It's been a very long time since we celebrated Christmas together. I would really like to do some good cooking for you, like I used to when you lived here.'

'I have to be back in the office,' I said, almost believing in those words myself. 'And, I can't change the ticket now, mom, I didn't opt for a flexible ticket.'

She was leaning against the wall, an inch outside my bedroom's door, as if scared to cross into my territory, her face wrinkled and tired from the lack of sleep. 'I don't understand why you would book your ticket for today. I really don't understand.' She continued in a weak, patronizing voice, clearly unconvinced by my reasoning.

I felt she had by now given up any hopes that I would ever become the daughter she had so much struggled to raise.

'Sorry, mom.' I said, looking at the floor, suddenly feeling guilty. 'I didn't think about it. I just booked the ticket to Dubai with the intention to get back to the office as soon as possible. I have got stuff waiting for me there.'

'I see.' She nodded her head with disbelief and looked me straight in the eye. 'But, what do you think I come to Dubai for Christmas and spend some time with you?'

She said the last few words slowly, as if whispering a secret.

'Sure, this sounds brilliant.' I jumped; happy that she had thought of such thing. 'I will book your ticket now. You will love it there, mom, I am sure, it's an amazing place! Finally, something we can both look forward to.'

'Great, sounds like we have a plan.' She smiled and walked into the room to give me a warm embrace that smelled so much like love.

London, 21 December 2018

Reza had asked me to fly through London on the way back to Dubai. He wanted to discuss how the 'New Millennium' project was getting on. At 3:00 p.m., I was waiting outside his office, but he was nowhere to be found. The secretary of the engineering department told me that he had called off sick and was expected to be back in the office in January.

It really upset me that he had not told me about it earlier, but I had to catch up with so much work, that I didn't really mind it that much. I had a few hours to spare before departing for Dubai in the evening, so I could use the time to study the material for the next day's annual progress meeting with the client. Liam would chair that meeting, so I had to read through the latest reports, in case he wanted to ask something beforehand.

I sat at my old desk which looked very different now. Someone had used the desk since I had moved to Dubai and they had left a piece of themselves there. I could see that there were plenty of rulers scattered around the desk and many color markers and pens squashed inside a cup that bore the company logo. It was likely that an AutoCAD drafter had been sitting there.

I took the cup closer to get a pen and suddenly realized that there was also one black and yellow stripped pencil squashed between markers. I took the little faceless soldier on my palm and looked at it, carefully checking all its edges and corners. The letter C had been carved on its skin which confirmed my suspicions that it was one of my dear pencils.

Without wasting another second, I put the pencil into my bag. Then I started to work on my laptop.

Time after time I glanced at the cup, its rainbow color markers humming with joy. Something didn't feel quite right, though. Out of the blue, an odd feeling of anxiety had started to build up in my stomach.

I took the pencil out of the bag and placed it back inside the cup. My soldier doesn't seem faceless anymore, I thought. He looks unique. He is unique, I concluded, just like what Liam had called me the first time we kissed outside my apartment door. We are all unique, I almost whispered, and realized that the anxiety butterflies in my stomach had suddenly disappeared.

I continued to read through the meeting presentation material, happy that I would soon be seeing Liam.

The next morning, by 8 a.m., I had landed in Dubai.

Meeting was set to start at 10:30 a.m. Because I was there earlier than everyone else, I had switched on my laptop and set up the power point on the wall screen. Before that, I had briefly gone through the meeting agenda. Now, I was waiting for the team to show up. In fact, I was waiting for one particular person to show up; my dear man.

The room almost filled up immediately, people sat down, opened their laptops and started to chat with each other. I saw him enter the room in quick pace, clean and fresh, full of confidence. The room instantly filled with energy.

'All right, did you have a good flight?' He said as he wrote the date on his notebook.

'Yes, I did', I answered softly, looking at Max across the table. 'Are you all set with the presentation?'

'Yes, all ready.' He said in higher voice, his confidence pumped up.

'Great, if you wish, I could deliver the second part of the presentation, which talks about the geotechnical results we have gathered. I could expand a bit more on the methodology we use on site.' I said and opened the project notes I had brought with me.

'Sure', He replied with a firm voice, looking across the table at the client representative sitting next to Max and who seemed totally embroiled in the conversation the two of them were having.

I pretended to focus on my notebook screen, while Liam started reading through the slides of the presentation. I knew he would most likely present the second half of the presentation himself; he always did that. It looked better for the company to have the manager deliver the entire presentation, even if that meant no one else would get a chance to show what they were working on. I knew that wasn't quite right, but I never felt as if he was not giving me space.

He was the manager; he had the right to take over when he deemed it appropriate. I would be pleased if the messages delivered during the meeting were clear enough for me to not have to intervene.

By 1:00 p.m. the meeting was over. As I was wrapping up the files in the conference room, Max came over to me. He seemed tired and bored.

'I am so happy this meeting is over. I was half asleep, to be honest with you. Thankfully Liam had it all under control so we could just hibernate in our seats.'

I raised a faint smile, almost certain that I had spotted some sarcasm in his words.

"Shall we get some proper lunch outside? I cannot take any more sandwiches. I bet you would also like to have something with more flavor after such a long flight.' He said and yawned with his mouth wide open.

'Yes, sure, give me a minute.' I said and walked out of the conference room. I placed the laptop and folders on my desk, took out the wallet from the hand luggage and looked around to locate Max.

He was still inside the conference room, smiling joyfully at his phone. Liam was standing a few feet away from Max, talking to clients.

I waved at Max, but he was too concentrated on his phone, so I started walking towards him.

Half-way through, I spotted Claire, the HR manager, emerging from the elevator, and heading towards the conference room. A large, pink bottle of champagne was clutched under her arm. Her eyes met mine and she smiled in a cheeky way, as if to say she was about to do something.

I slowed my pace and let her enter the room first. She looked around and then, when she found who she was looking for, smiled at him and slowly revealed the bottle of champagne that she had brought with her.

Liam smiled back at Claire, nodding lightly as if to say: Okay, go with it!

Not knowing what to think, I just stood there numb. 'What on earth is going on?' I thought to myself, as Max, finally realized I was there. He came closer, looking clearly excited, and whispered to my ear. 'Well, well, the company has finally decided to splurge and wrap up the meeting properly. Finally, some champagne to celebrate the good progress of the project. Quick Sharron, we don't want to miss the boat.' He said and walked towards Claire.

I followed him just as Claire asked us all to keep quiet for a few minutes. She then went on to make a pompous speech about the progress of the project. Among other things, she made a synopsis of the meeting outcomes and then congratulated Liam for his work on the project and wished him good luck in his pastures new.

Max turned around to face me, clearly baffled by what was going on.

I did not really comprehend what I had just heard; I just looked out for Liam.

Once he saw me, he waved, smiling briefly with reassurance.

Claire eventually explained that Liam was moving back to London as he had been promoted for his performance on the "New Millennium" project. He would soon become the new Middle East projects manager.

Shortly after the speech was over and people were busy enjoying their drinks, I sneaked back to my desk and sent out a quick email to HR Department saying that I would take the rest of the day off due to jet lag.

Liam was still busy talking to people when I left the building, so he probably didn't realize I was leaving.

In reality, I thought that he did realize I was leaving, but he just didn't want to confront me in front of everyone else.

He probably thought it was wiser to speak in private. He wouldn't want to risk his reputation by being seen as having a private argument with me. He was quite cautious when it came to such things. His work was to never be muddled up with his private life – that was something I had been made aware of since the very start of the relationship.

He did text me an hour later, saying that he would come to my apartment to explain it all. He also wrote that he loved me. He didn't say that he was sorry for anything though.

It was late in the afternoon when Liam finally came over to my apartment. He looked tired but strangely excited.

Once he closed the door behind him, he gave me a long hug and then a soft kiss on the lips. He took my face into his hands and said that he had missed me. He then handed me over a small paper bag with a Christmas gift inside, which I placed on the table without opening it.

I asked him to sit down. Since I had arrived home, I had taken a shower, put on my pajamas and then crashed to bed hoping to get some sleep. I was used to bad news, so Claire's speech had not particularly surprised me, it had just added more anxiety to my otherwise dull day. Now that I had seen it all, I felt that what didn't kill me would only make me stronger. Or something like that. I don't know why I felt like that. Maybe it is true what they say, once you hit rock bottom, you can only stay there, it can't get any worse.

I noticed that Liam was getting impatient, he wanted to say things, so I decided to not say anything but let him talk first.

'Sharrie, I'm sorry I didn't tell you about it earlier, but you were so involved with the things back home that I didn't want to further distress you. Every time we spoke on the phone, I thought about telling you, but you seemed so drained by what was going on back home.

I thought it was best to explain how things stand in person... And I am really sorry for what happened this morning, I had no idea about that joke of a speech they had planned.' He blurted nervously with his soft, white hands shaking as they moved incautiously in the air.

I looked at him and nodded in silence.

'It was wrong to break the news like that to you, and it was also unfair to me as I haven't signed the contract yet.' He said defensively.

'So, you are not leaving?' I asked, puzzled, my eyes begging for it to have all been a huge misunderstanding.

'Listen, I have only said yes in principle, but I just want you to know that I had both of us in mind when taking that decision.' He said hurriedly and came closer to me.

'What do you mean?' I asked, even more puzzled. 'I am happy here, I have you, I have got friends and I like the work. Why move back?'

'Because things are not as good as they look.' He said in a serious tone. 'Do you know why Reza was not in the office yesterday? Because they are shutting down the geotechnical department in London. Soon, Reza and yourself will be out of work. The company has decided to subcontract all the geotechnical assessments, as it is much cheaper that way.'

My heart sank. All that I had worked for the last year, all my efforts had been in vain.

'I had a lengthy chat with Reza about it,' He continued. 'There is nothing he could have done that could have saved the department. It was a top management decision. Having said that, there may be an opportunity to shift you to a different department over there, like structures or project engineering, if you wished to stay with the company. It is just a few of you in the geotechnical department, so I am sure they could fit you guys somewhere.'

'I see.' I muttered in pain. 'But I don't really want to go back. I don't want to be sitting at my old desk anymore. I wouldn't be able to stand that.' I confessed. 'I will be looking for a job over here.'

'No, no, you are coming back with me.' He said full of confidence. 'We are leaving together.'

'Well, I am not.' I said calmly. I don't want to move back to London. I can't really go back there. I can't really explain it to you, but it is impossible for me to go back there. I prefer to be made redundant while working here.'

'But now things are different, darling.' He said and took my hands into his. 'We will be together this time. All your battles are mine, and mine are yours, remember? It will be a solid start for us, we can settle there for good. You know we can't keep doing what we are doing now, I am your manager after all. It will be better if we work in different departments. This way we can hang out in the open.'

'I am sorry. I am not moving back there.' I said. 'You should have asked me, if you wanted me to come with you.'

'I thought I made myself clear as to why I didn't tell you beforehand.' Liam frowned and let go of my hands. 'Is this what this is all about? Not telling you in advance? You don't need to act like a spoiled girl and kick a fuss about it. All I did, I did for both of us.'

'I thought this was just a good career move for you. Why would it be good for me? You have no idea what I have been through living alone over there.' I snapped loudly.

'Well, tell me then.' He said patiently. 'Why don't you just open up and tell me everything about back home, about what made you leave? Tell me, for God's sake. How on earth are we going to get anywhere if we don't start sharing what troubles us?'

'Well, you go first, I am not ready yet.' I said. 'And you seemed patient enough all this time. Why all the sudden rush? Are you going to fix my problems and have me packaged back to London with you? That is what you are good at, finding solutions day in, day out. It is not going to work like that with me, I am afraid. I just don't want to be reminded of the past. I just want to let it go and live this bloody life in peace.'

'I know what this is all about,' He said calmly and stood up with his back turned on me. He looked outside the balcony glass window, which looked at Dubai's main highway. The warm, golden lights from the cars were shyly piercing his fragile, icy blue eyes. He concentrated his look somewhere, seemingly overwhelmed by that symphony of lights dancing peacefully into his irises.

He then took a deep breath and continued in a mourning tone. 'It seems to me that your mission in life is to sabotage any efforts for happiness. You have set yourself up to bury deep down the misery that you have created. If you want to stay there, fine, but if you ever want to give yourself a second chance, if you want to push yourself up the ditch, then give me a call. And I promise you, I will pick it up. But only then.'

He then turned around and without looking at me, walked out.

It is strange how someone can deal with loss. I had, in the blink of an eye, lost the person I loved the most in the entire world. And yet, in that empty, cold apartment, I felt no loneliness or anxiety. I didn't even feel sadness. I just felt relieved.

Maybe it was true that all I wanted was to sabotage anything good from ever happening to me. Because what had just happened felt so very much foreseen.

I opened the balcony door and let the warm evening air walk into the air-conditioned apartment.

And then, I walked outside, breathing in the warm air with my lungs fully open, thinking that there never was hope for us as a couple anyways.

After a while, I headed back to the kitchen to get myself a glass of wine. I walked lethargically past a giant, Moroccan mirror, hanging on the wall that separated the kitchen from the living room, and for some reason, I saw a white reflection blinking at me from within the mirror. I looked at it again, and again, until I realized that I was actually looking at Anthony's ravaged face.

Great Falls Town, 31 December 2007

Why do all good things come to an end?

Christie never made it to my mother's house. That night was the very last time I saw her. She was simply gone; gone forever from my small, provincial life. She was gone to never return, to never explain or apologize for her decision.

She was gone without saying goodbye, without bothering to write two lines to me. And I don't know what it was that hurt me the most; her decision to leave or her arrogance to not tell me beforehand.

For years and years, I tried to console myself by thinking that she was living in a distant place which could not be reached. And there, I pictured her busy; she had always been busy - so she had to be doing things; setting up businesses, doing charity work or dating good looking guys. Either way, she was busy living her life, her dreams and passions. Clearly, she was too busy to ever call on me.

I was certain that Christie would do better than me, whatever it was that she had planned to do. So, if I were to ever meet her again, I knew that she would talk for hours on end about her achievements, and I would stare at her as she spoke, baffled by her stories, anxious to hear it all there and then. And as she would talk, I would silently long to suddenly jump over and hug her, crying in silence behind her soft back. But I would refrain from doing so because I wouldn't want to spoil the moment, of course.

After she would talk forever about herself like she used to as a child, she would eventually ask things about me. I would be scared to say anything that would hint to how messed up my life had been. So, I would make up things about myself too; I would say I had a good-looking boyfriend and a successful career overseas. I would say I hadn't thought of Great Falls Town much, as I had been busy building up my dreams. And I would also tell her that I hadn't missed anything from high school, as life was now too fast tracked to even remember those years.

And then she would smile, laugh occasionally at my silly answers and instantaneously become serious at the next question she had planned to ask.

So, you see, I had imagined all sorts of conversations with her; all sorts of questions and answers we would ask one another. I had even imagined how at the end Christie would say she would like to stay longer but had a flight to catch and would offer to pay as she always used to, but this time, I would insist and have the bill myself.

And then, as she would stand up and give me a quick kiss on the cheek; a formality that all good old friends do in such occasions, and which always leaves you with a bittersweet feeling of not really knowing your old friend anymore, as with time, high school friends grow old and grow apart as they say – I would realize that something wasn't stacking up. Then I would rehearse another, more convincing meeting in my mind.

In reality, despite her words, I would have still noticed the small things; the fact that her blazer was the same as ten years ago, or that she didn't have a car parked in the restaurant car park, or that the hot chocolate still left stains on her upper lip, as it used to when she was fifteen years old.

It would be all these things, but above all, it would be her face that would give her away. Her face was too young; too untroubled by the toxic pollution of this life to ever sustain that line of events.

So, regardless of editing the meeting in my mind repeatedly, I would not be able to change her beautiful face, because that is how I remembered her and how she would always be.

On the night of December 31, I waited in vain for Christie to return from the Marriott hotel.

Initially, I was angry at her, so I locked myself in the room, certain that I would not get out even if she came knocking at my door, begging me to join them at the dinner table.

But when the clock started ticking slowly towards dawn and grandma, mother and Bobby were long gone to sleep after a lonely dinner between the three of us, my anger subsided into a feeling of betrayal. I was now feeling that Christie had chosen Anthony over our friendship; she had chosen someone she barely knew over me.

By 5:00 a.m. I was so exhausted of looking outside of my room's window for a glimpse of hers that the nausea had become bigger and the pain at the back of my head had become unbearable. I got out of the room and told mother I wasn't feeling well.

She immediately packed my hospital bag and we stormed off to A&E. After a number of checks, I was re-admitted to the hospital that same morning.

I didn't hear back from Christie that day. I had not called her the previous night and wasn't planning to do it later either. She had to call first; she was the one that had let me down.

I thought over the years that if I had called her that night, she could still be with us. But I didn't, and I had to live with that for the rest of my life.

What exactly happened that night did not matter much, as regardless of the details, the outcome couldn't change. She wasn't coming back. Period. She wasn't ever coming back.

So, in that sense, it didn't matter either that no one actually found out what happened that night.

Different people said different things over the years and different witnesses changed their minds too, so the puzzle eventually turned into a labyrinth from where no light was to ever come out. And to be fair, I never dived too deep into that labyrinth because I knew, the more I searched, the more I would hate the people around her, people I loved deeply.

But I did have a summary of what happened that night, put together in chronological order by Great Falls Town's local newspaper. The story made the first page for many newspapers, but most of the stuff reported was pure speculation.

The extract, which was cut out from the newspaper was mailed to me by Nick, four years after Christie's loss. I never understood why he felt he had to mail me that summary of events. Perhaps, he thought, it would make me feel better somehow. It really had the opposite effect.

The summary of events was something like this:

"On the evening of December 31, 2007, at 7:05 p.m. Christie Jones was spotted entering the Marriott Hotel. She was greeted by Anthony McAlester at the front lobby of the hotel.

At 7:45 p.m., Vince Jones was seen entering the front lobby of the Marriott Hotel. At 7:50 p.m., Vince

Jones and Anthony McAlester were seen altercating loudly. Vince and Christie Jones were later seen leaving the hotel in their green truck. This happened circa 8:10 p.m.

At 8:40 p.m., staff at Restaurant Paradise admitted to have witnessed a row between Vince and Christie Jones. Initially the two had been shouting loudly and throwing things at one another. Staff witnessed that Vince Jones had beaten Christie; he had slapped her in the face, pulled her hair and punched her in the stomach. He had thrown a chair at her and as a result her left leg was seen to be heavily bruised.

Staff had intervened to stop the fight and had neutralized Vince Jones who had continued to scream to be left alone with his daughter.

Christie was seen leaving the restaurant at around 9:20 p.m. She was neither wearing her coat nor carrying her phone with her.

Later in the evening, she was seen entering the Lion Pub at 9:45 p.m. where she was allowed inside, regardless of being under age. Witnesses at the pub said she looked anxious. Christie Jones was spotted drinking alcohol before leaving the pub at about 2:00 a.m. on January 1.

In the morning of January 1, Christie Jones was found by Vince Jones, in the back garden of their home. All the gathered evidence suggested to suicide by hanging..."

Vince Jones came to see me at the hospital on January 3. By that time, I was feeling better, however I was still very much upset with Christie. She had not called, and even when I had tried to call her a day earlier, her phone had been switched off.

It was late in the evening when Vince entered the hospital room and I was half asleep when he first talked to me. He did not say much; he swiftly apologized to mother for the late visit and then asked if I was feeling better.

I reassured him I was well. At that point, I didn't really care about the head pain, I was so angry with Christie that my mind was nonstop thinking of how ruthless and infidel she had been towards me.

I asked Mr. Jones if Christie knew I were in hospital and he did say that she knew and she would come to see me very soon. Then, as he was about to say something else, one of the nurses entered the room and he stood there silent, looking at how she administered my medication.

Then he left swiftly, but before doing so, gave me a long kiss on the forehead.

I didn't think much of that visit. Yes, it was late in the night when Mr. Jones decided to pop in, but he was a busy man and that time of year, he had a lot of work at the restaurant. I was only thinking of Christie. She knew I were in hospital, so she had to be coming to see me very soon.

It happened on the evening of January 6, when I was still in hospital. That is the time I found out what had happened to Christie.

The consultant had said I would be discharged in two to three days, if the tests continued to show steady results, so I was counting the minutes until I would be out of there. Christie had not yet called me; it was so much unlike her to continue with an old, silly grudge.

I went outside the room to secretly pick a coke can from the vending machine at the pediatrics outpatients waiting area, which happened to be just a few doors down my room. I used to do that when mother would go to the canteen to have dinner.

It remained vivid in my mind for many years the way the two ladies sitting by the vending machine talked about what had happened to Christie; it sounded just like the rest of the town's hot daily gossip. Painless and crude.

I asked them again for the girl's name, after hearing what they had just said, and they repeated it. And then they effortlessly described the details of what had happened to the poor girl.

Dear God, they did not spare me any details; stuff I wish I had never known. They went on and on, so brutally honest with their words, so intrusive and malicious at the same time.

But this is what people did when they talked about strangers, I thought. A stranger's tragedy was not a real tragedy; it was just another story you saw on the news. We all talked about it even though we wished bad things did not happen to people. Deep inside though, we dehumanized that stranger on purpose, because we knew that it felt better to speak up the gossip than respect their tragedy in silence.

I put on mother's coat, got some cash off her wallet and left the hospital running.

In less than an hour, the taxi I had managed to pick outside the hospital, had stopped in front of Christie's house.

The snow that had fallen earlier in the day had covered the grass at the front garden by a few inches, but I could still see it all; the flowers, the cards and the extinguished candles, now slowly disappearing beneath the white layers of snow.

I rushed to the house, but the front door was locked, so I walked to the rear garden. And there, flashes of images appeared to me. I could now see how it all happened, what her last few hours had been like.

Breathless, I lied down under the tree, looking at the sky above me; thinking I would soon wake up.

I submerged myself deep under the snow, until I could feel no more the pain at the back of my head. And I watched patiently above me, the branches and leaves of that old fig tree dance slowly with the stars in the sky.

Dubai, 24 December 2018

Mother arrived in Dubai on December 24. She had planned to celebrate Christmas and the New Year with me and leave on January 12.

Despite feeling devastated by the recent breakup with Liam, I wanted her to enjoy the holidays. So, I told myself I had to give it all for her to feel happy, at least for once.

We toured the city, visited all possible museums, skyscrapers and entertainment parks.

We rode on camels across the desert, went shopping in the countless malls and even had dinners on the palm islands.

She was happy, or at least, that was my impression of her.

The night before her flight back home, we went out to have dinner at a restaurant overlooking the sea. Because she would leave the next day, she was slightly melancholic. She drank her wine slowly, enjoying the warm breeze from the sea that played lazily with her thin, grey hair.

At one point, she looked at me straight in the eye and said that something was off. In Vermont, I had seemed happier, more energetic, she said. Now I looked different, not so excited with things. She asked if something had changed. I did have a ready response in my tongue, but this time, I decided I wanted to tell her the truth.

I said that I had broken up recently. I had lost the person who I thought had saved me; the one that had made my heart pound with excitement every second of the day. I told her that he had broken up with me because I was scared to move on, to change my skin.

Mother was devastated. But strangely, she didn't look surprised.

She then said something that completely astonished me. She said that no one could save me. Not a lover hero, not Bobby, not even her. She said that I didn't need to be saved because there was nothing to be saved from. I just had to love myself a tiny bit more.

She then asked for me to go back home. She said we could move town, or even state.

I listened and listened and then told her I would think about.

At the airport, before she left, she asked again.

I finally decided to not fool her anymore. I told her I would never go back, but that wasn't because I was running away from home, I was just happier away.

She looked sad. She pulled herself quickly though and kissed me hard on the cheek. She said she would call me after landing.

It felt as if mother was fearful of me. She might have been, but I wasn't. Not anymore.

Great Falls Town, 8 January 2008

It is really hard to stay calm under snow. The cold gets to you. It gets to your heart that pumps crazily in vain and to your muscles that ache painfully until they go numb. It gets to your head that is constantly telling you to get up and run for your life.

Luckily for me, it all ended very soon.

I had been lying under snow for about thirty minutes when Mr. Jones found me. Lisa had been barking madly so he had left the house to check what was going on.

Fortunately, I woke up when Lisa stepped on me. Her barking was so loud that it did feel like a calling, a calling from above to get up.

Mr. Jones fell on his knees and frantically cleaned the snow above and around me. He then carried me back to his house. He submerged me into a hot bath and later changed me into Christie's pajamas.

I never forgot that. Not the clothes, no, the smell of them, the smell of Christie.

A few minutes later, when I was fully conscious, Mr. Jones dragged the old, noisy couch next to the fireplace, handed me a hot cup of tea and told me to sit there and finish it. These were the only words he blurted to me that night.

Mother arrived after fifteen minutes. She would have driven like a bullet on the icy roads to make it to Mr. Jones's house that quick. She screamed between tears when she saw me clutched into the couch, wrapped under a heavy blanket that only revealed my head.

She took my hands into hers and in an apologetic tone murmured, 'Why Sharrie, why?'

Facing mother was difficult for me, though I had no strength to say anything back to her. I knew she was sad beyond words; she was also deeply disappointed that I had done such thing. I had let her down, fully and completely and there was no way I could ever change that.

We drove back to the hospital shortly afterwards. Mother never stopped crying on the wheel, even though the road ahead of us was bumpy due to large patches of snow and ice that had fallen during the day.

Mr. Jones was sat at the back of the car with me. He held me tightly under the warm blanket with his large hands constantly trembling and his breath sounding heavy, almost claustrophobic.

Squashed like that, under his shaky, big hands, I felt the closest I had been to Christie since she was gone.

Once again, I was back in the hospital, back to the same room. This time more tubes were piercing my body – long snakes that bit me each time I endeavored to move. I was also getting inhalers every four hours. I had caught pneumonia.

When the doctors finally managed to complete all the necessary checks and confirmed that I was out of danger, mother left the room to speak to Mr. Jones. He had been by her side, all this time. Mother wanted to know the details, why and how the whole thing happened.

Around midnight, Mr. Jones left the hospital. Before leaving, he asked mother if she wanted anything from the store. Mother said she wanted nothing. She kindly asked to keep the incident private though. Mr. Jones nodded without saying a word.

All night, mother wept and wept in silence. I don't know if it was more because of what I had attempted to do, or because the entire world would learn about it in the morning. You see, she knew that once you tried to kill yourself and people knew of it, they would expect you to somehow finish the work you had started. There was no going back after that.

Unless something major happened to you… Something that raised their empathy. Something that in a way gave them a reason to justify your future existence. And I, for better or worse, was given that.

On the morning of January 9, exactly twelve hours after I had lied down in the frozen garden of his home, Vince Jones was found dead in the very same place. He had shot himself in the head.

Epilogue

My entire life revolved around finding the WHY, the reason why Mr. Jones did what he did.

I never managed to find out that WHY.

When I became an adult, people most of whom therapists, told me that he had done what he had done because he had wanted no one else to repeat Christie's actions. By saying no one else, I believe they were referring to me.

According to them, Mr. Jones had thought that by taking his own life he had provided closure to Christie's death. He had paid for what he had done with his own life. A life for a life.

The weird thing in all of this is that none of the people involved in that tragedy really found closure because of what he did.

Tom and Nick both left town soon after what happened. They felt guilty for not having intervened to keep Christie safe during that mad fight Christie and Mr. Jones had on New Year's Eve.

Mrs. Elliott, whose big red mouth haunted me for years, initially moved to work at a different restaurant in town. For years, she denied that it was her who told Mr. Jones where Christie had been that night. Everyone supposed it had been me.

Six years ago, she finally admitted to Tom that she had heard Christie's phone call with Anthony McAlester on the night of New Year's Eve where they had agreed to meet up for two hours at the Marriott Hotel, before he would drop her to my mother's house.

Mrs. Elliott had noticed Christie's changed behavior those last few weeks. She had seen her take out large sums of money from the cashier machine and place it in her school purse. That had made her suspicious that someone was using Christie's kind heart.

So, she had decided to tell Mr. Jones about Christie meeting up with a boyfriend at the Marriott hotel that night, purely out of concern for her.

I never heard from Mrs. Elliott. After Christie's loss, she never spoke to anyone associated with the Jones family.

I heard from mother that she retired in 2016. She continued to live in her apartment, in the outskirts of Great Falls Town, alone, until she passed away from a stroke last winter.

As for myself, all that was left after the events was a spiral of guilt and self-loathing which spun me around for years. I felt guilty for what had happened to Christie, and I felt even more so for having driven Mr. Jones to his death. All my life, I believed that I was a mere domino, which had just been hit and was expected to fall to the ground just like the rest before had.

The thing was, Mr. Jones's death did not liberate me; it did not provide closure, if that was what he had in mind. It didn't make me miss Christie any less. It didn't make me blame myself any less either.

It just made me feel completely and utterly responsible for his death. And as a child, that haunted me more than Christie's loss.

Dubai, April 2019

Winter in Dubai came to an end early, and so did my time as an expat there.

I was now sat on a plane back to London, hoping to sign off a contract with the company for a permanent position in Dubai. I had agreed to all the details over the phone and was hoping that the meeting would be straightforward, i.e. signing a few papers and then heading straight back to Dubai.

The geotechnical department had been closed down in February. Everyone in the team, including Reza, had accepted similar roles in other departments. Finally, everyone seemed to be settled.

As far as I was concerned, the last few months had been difficult, but surprisingly bearable.

The "New Millennium" project, being fast track, had kept me busy. During the day, I had little time to think of anything else but work. The nights were more difficult, but still manageable. I would often go out with Amir and the rest of the operations team to local pubs to have a spirit drink.

I had even made a few local friends, thanks to Amir's social skills, and during weekends, I would often join them to the movies, malls or restaurants.

Despite feeling generally upbeat, I had continued to miss Liam. I missed him every single day, every single hour of the day. I missed his smell, his soft hands, the icy blue eyes that reminded me of Great Falls Town's deep blue springs.

I missed the little conversations we had together; the things he used to say that made me want to become a better human being and change the world.

I missed sleeping by his side and then waking up to see him next to me.

I missed a million things about him, but above all, I missed his friendship.

The truth was, that evening at my apartment, when he had so bluntly told me that I had set myself up for failure, had been a real game changer for me.

Right after he had said those words, I had realized that I was none of that. I might not have been the success story he had wanted me to become, but I was a strong, resilient human being who wouldn't give up on herself.

And, funnily, it was also only then that I realized that it hadn't really been Liam who had saved me, it had been myself. I had saved myself because I had opted for change rather than stagnation. I had saved myself because I was the only one who could do it and had done it by changing my way of life. No superhero could do that but me. "There was nothing to be saved from. You just need to love yourself a tiny bit more," my mother had said, and was right.

I had finally understood that I saved myself, because I started to love myself above and beyond anyone else.

When Liam left the apartment that night, I headed to the fridge to get a glass of wine.

The truth was, I had stopped drinking alcohol, since I had started going out with Liam. I used to keep the bottle of wine in the fridge in case I wanted to do something stupid with myself.

And when I walked past that Moroccan mirror and saw Anthony's ravaged face looking at me, I understood that I was not the only one who suffered. The world was full of pain, full of loss, just like that taxi man who had lost his whole family and prayed for them every single day. He celebrated their lives by living the life that they had not had a chance to live.

Yet, I still headed to the fridge, this time not to drink the bottle, but to smash it down on the sink.

And then after doing that, triumphant and relieved, I opened the small paper bag that Liam had brought for me.

There was a set of lipsticks inside and a box of black and yellow striped pencils.

The card read: "Merry Christmas, my love. Please wear lipstick more often, it looks good on you. p.s. Sorry I spilled coffee over your dear pencils, here is a new set. Love Liam".

I laid the pencils on the couch, admiring the stripes in silence, as a faint smile rose on my face.

Since Liam had moved back to London, he had returned to the office in Dubai a few times, primarily to conduct high level meetings with the clients and the new manager that had replaced him.

We spoke briefly. He apologized for his words that night and said that he missed me. He further asked if I had changed my mind about moving back to London with him.

I said no, and as a result we hadn't spoken a lot after that.

Now that I was on the plane and had plenty of time to think, I had decided to ask him out.

This time, I would bring out all the skeletons from the cupboard and lay them all in front of him. It was going to be his take or leave, the full truth or nothing.

I was so much hoping for him to say yes, to accept me the way I was, the weird, introvert crackpot, who kept black and yellow striped pencils at the edge of her desk and who always found joy in the burning sun.

But I had to wait for a few more hours until I met him to know for sure. For now, I was happy to watch the black sky full of sparkling diamond stars, that shone with such bright light which reminded me that I was not alone here and never would be. Because as Christie often said, "God always travels with light and you need to see it, for him to see you."